No Longer Sings
the Brown Thrush

No Longer Sings the Brown Thrush

Mary Blair Immel

*Farmers in southern Illinois said that
after the assassination of Abraham
Lincoln the brown thrush quit singing*

CBP Press
St. Louis, Missouri

Library of Congress Cataloging-in-Publication Data

Immel, Mary Blair.
   No longer sings the brown thrush / by Mary Blair Immel.
     p. cm.
   Summary: After her father is killed in battle in 1864, twelve-year-
old Tildy and her family reluctantly move to Maryland where Tildy
learns of a plot to assassinate President Lincoln.
   ISBN 0-8272-2509-1 : $11.95
   1. Lincoln, Abraham, 1809-1865—Assassination—Juvenile fiction.
[1. Lincoln, Abraham, 1809-1865—Assassination—Fiction. 2. United
States—History—Civil War, 1861-1865—Fiction.]   I. Title.
PZ7.I34No   1988
[Fic]—dc19   87-27354
                                               CIP
                                              AC

Illustrations by Patrice Holt.

Printed in the United States of America

Dedicated to
Polly, Katja, Becky, Chena, Andi
—my cup runneth over—

Author's Note

Surrattsville really existed. It has now been renamed Clinton, Maryland. Surratt's Tavern is now a museum open to the public. The Surratt family as well as John Wilkes Booth, who killed Abraham Lincoln, were all real people.

Tildy and the rest of the people in this book are make-believe.

It is known that there were various groups who plotted to kidnap President Lincoln.

1

Vinsontown, Indiana
July, 1864

Every day for the past week, Tildy Graham had
checked carefully to see if the letter addressed to Surrattsville, Maryland was still on the table next to Mother's
big family Bible. As soon as Tildy saw that the letter had
not yet been mailed, she breathed a prayer of thankful-
ness. It meant she was safe for a little while longer.

Tildy's mother had written that letter on the terrible
night when the bad news about Papa had been delivered.
Tildy knew that if she lived to be one hundred years old,
she would remember clear as creek water how Mr.
Scroggins from the train depot had come out to the
Graham farmhouse, along with Reverend Martin from
the Christian Church.

It had been when her mother and Tildy and Elizabeth
and little Louisa were eating supper that they had heard
someone knocking on the door. Seeing Mr. Scroggins
and Reverend Martin standing there together like that
and the look on their faces, Tildy had known what was
wrong before either of the men could say a word.

"I'm sorry to have to be the one to tell you," Mr.
Scroggins had said. "But this message came across on
the telegraph wire just a short time ago."

Mr. Scroggins had handed a piece of paper to Mother. Tildy remembered thinking at that moment that her mother seemed like one of the slender young saplings that she and Papa had planted in the lane just before he left. Their trunks seemed so slight and trembly when caught by a sudden gust of chill wind. They had been bent almost to the ground but they had held through the storm. Tildy watched as Mother had read the words written on the piece of paper. Tildy had seen her mother sway noticeably and put out her hand to steady herself, but she didn't break.

"There was a battle down in Georgia," Mr. Scroggins had explained. "A place called Kennesaw Mountain. Happened on the twenty-seventh of June."

Tildy was pretty sure that neither of her younger sisters, eight-year-old Elizabeth nor three-year-old Louisa, had really understood what Mr. Scroggins was saying. It was probably the way Mother's face got as white as the cambric collar on her dress. Or, maybe it was the way the room was suddenly too quiet and everybody stood looking at everybody else. Whatever it was, both of the younger Graham sisters had started to cry at once. Then, Reverend Martin had begun to pray out loud asking God's comfort at the loss of Jeremiah Graham, husband and father.

Perhaps it was because Tildy and her mother were so busy comforting Elizabeth and Louisa, getting them put to bed and lulling them to sleep, that their own tears were held back for much later that night.

Tildy's own grief seemed doubly bitter. She had lost her father and that meant that the family was probably going to lose this farm. Next to her family, Tildy thought she loved this farm more than anything else. There wasn't a foot of ground that she and her father hadn't walked over and worked together since they filed their claim on it. Papa's love for this land had made it seem a part of him. Even when he was not with her, just working the land made Tildy feel close to him. Losing this farm would be like losing Papa all over again.

Try as she might, Tildy could not put the memory of that awful evening out of her mind. She remembered how Mr. Scroggins had said that Papa was brave to go with the Union army when lots of other men paid a bounty to have someone else go in their place. Mr. Scroggins also said that a medal for Papa would be coming. And Reverend Martin said that it was a blessing that Papa had not lingered in pain for days as so many of the wounded men did. After they had said all of that, the two men left. As she watched them go, Tildy had felt almost as sorry for them as she did for herself. It must have been hard for them to bring such news.

When the men had gone, Mother had stood looking around the room, not saying a word. Then, after a little bit she had gone to the black walnut sewing stand that Papa had made for her one Christmas. Mother had rummaged about among the sewing scraps and finally found a piece of heavy grosgrain ribbon. Then Mother had picked up the picture of Papa that stood on the mantle and draped the heavy black ribbon over it.

Finally, Mother had looked at Tildy and said, "I know what you're thinking, Tildy, but we simply cannot stay here on the farm without your father. Things might be different if there had been some sons to help, but a woman with three young daughters. . . ."

Tildy blinked back the tears that wanted to spill over. "Papa always said that I could do as much work around this place as any boy he ever knew could do."

Mother nodded. "That's true, Tildy. I don't deny that, but we've got to face facts. I cannot take your father's place with the heavy work, and one twelve-year-old girl cannot keep a farm going all by herself."

"We've done all right so far," Tildy insisted.

"Just barely," Mother said. "And that was because we had hope to keep us going . . . the hope that your father would be back someday. Now that's gone."

"The neighbors helped us, too," Tildy blurted out before she realized that argument was not helping her case.

"We can't keep on accepting that kind of help. Your father wouldn't have wanted that. Folks have got their own work to do without adding ours to their burden."

Tildy looked at her father's picture on the mantle as though she would find the answer there. How handsome he looked in his dark blue kersey uniform with the sergeant's stripes on the sleeve. His cap had been forced down over his thick, wavy, dark hair. He seemed to have been trying to strike a serious pose, as befit a Union soldier, but no matter how firmly he set his lips, he could do nothing about his eyes. His eyes always sparkled with the love of life, his joy at everything he saw. Papa simply couldn't look serious at all. He looked as though he were bursting with some wonderful secret about living and what it meant.

10

How proud Tildy had been of her father. She remembered the day he had left Vinsontown. She also remembered the words he had called to her from the train as it pulled out of the station. "Live up to your name, Tildy. Do the very best you can. You won't be happy doing less."

Living up to her name was a special secret Tildy and her father shared. She wasn't sure that Papa had told Mother why he had chosen the name Matilda for his firstborn daughter. But, as soon as Tildy had been old enough to understand, Papa had read to her from *A Child's History of England* about the brave Matilda. It seemed to Tildy that she could never hear enough of that story. As a little girl she begged over and over for Papa to read once more about the strong queen who had fought to save her crown from the false barons who had betrayed her.

Tildy had been wide-eyed at the account of Queen Matilda being besieged in the castle at Oxford. Even more exciting was the way Matilda managed to escape through the cold winter snowstorm with only three loyal knights to help her. They had camouflaged themselves by dressing all in white so that they could slip past the enemy. And, no matter how often she heard the story, she always wept at the end because Matilda had not won out at last.

"It's not fair, Papa," Tildy would cry. "It's not fair."

Papa had told her, "The important thing was that Matilda had tried."

So, when Papa had reminded Tildy to do the best she could, it was a very special secret between them. It had made her more determined than ever to keep the farm going until Papa came home again.

Papa had bought this land in Indiana six years ago. Papa had explained to her that this farm was an everyday reminder to him of how lucky he was.

Sometimes Tildy thought she was the only one who really understood how much Papa loved this place. She thought about it a lot, especially in those days just after Papa left to be with the army. Tildy knew that some of the folks in Vinsontown thought he was foolish to go off like that.

Old Mr. Pettibone had said it out loud one day and Tildy had overheard, "He should have paid his bounty money and let some younger man go in his place."

Mr. Pettibone's four sons were all young men, but they stayed home to work their farm. They had paid their bounty money.

Tildy knew that those people in Vinsontown who criticized Papa had not stood with him in the fields on a spring morning as she had.

"Do you feel it, Tildy?" Papa had asked. "Can you feel the promise in the air? It's a blessing you must never take for granted."

Then Papa stooped down and picked up a handful of the rich, dark Indiana soil and let it run slowly through his fingers. It was almost an act of devotion on his part.

"It makes me feel a part of this place when I work the land," Papa said.

Tildy supposed the love for this country was so deep in Papa because he had not been born here. He had adopted it for his own. Papa had come to America from

England when he was only twelve years of age. His mother had died in England and his father died shortly after they arrived here.

"All I had was the shirt on my back and hope in my pocket," Papa liked to remind her.

In America he had worked at whatever odd jobs he could get. He chopped wood and kept the fires stoked for a blacksmith. He learned to hammer nails straight while working for a carpenter. But, it was when he was helping a farmer clear rocks out of a field that he knew he wanted to farm the land.

"In some ways I was a slave," Papa had told Tildy. "But I made up my mind that someday I would own some land of my own." Papa had explained why he had decided to join Mr. Lincoln's army. "You see, I knew that no matter how bad off I was now, things could get better for me. Once I saved enough money to buy my own land then I could have the say over my own life and how I lived it. But how could I enjoy that kind of freedom when I knew that there were men, women, and children who were slaves with no hope just because of the color of their skin? I would never feel right having the blessings of this country if I didn't try to help other folks get those same blessings. I figure I owe this country a debt and I've got to repay it. We each have to do what we know is right, whether other folks understand or agree with us or not."

Tildy understood what Papa was talking about even if some of the people in Vinsontown didn't. She wished he hadn't felt as though he had to go, but she loved him and was proud of him for doing it.

That was why every morning, when she would much rather have snuggled deeper into the warm covers, she climbed out of bed and splashed her face in the icy cold water brought up from the spring. It was why she worked in the fields under the hot sun until her clothing stuck to her body with perspiration and her back ached. Papa had his duty to do and she had hers. She was going to keep this place going until Papa got back and they could go on the way they had before. Tildy kept thinking about Queen Matilda. This farm was worth struggling for more than any crown.

That night when they heard about Kennesaw Mountain and Papa, Tildy had watched her mother drape Papa's likeness in black. The awful news that Mr. Scroggins and Reverend Martin brought did not seem real at that time.

Tildy had turned away from the picture when she heard Mother talking to her. She made herself listen to words that she did not want to hear.

"When your father first left for the army, your Aunt Rachel wrote and invited us to come and stay with her family in Maryland. I think maybe that is what we had best do now."

"But, Mother," Tildy argued. "Maryland is in the South. . . . they had slaves in Maryland and we don't hold with slavery."

"You know as well as I do that Maryland is a border state," Mother corrected her. "It is still a part of this Union."

"But they did have slaves there, didn't they?" Tildy pressed the point.

"I suppose some people did," Mother said.

"Did Uncle Caleb have slaves?"

"I don't know," Mother answered. "That's not the sort of thing that my sister and I write about in our letters to each other."

"Well, I don't think that Papa would approve of us moving into a household that believes in slavery. Slaveholders are the people the Union is fighting against."

"The Union is fighting to get rid of an evil system, Tildy," Mother said. "Papa wouldn't want you to hate someone just because they had an idea we don't think is right. Uncle Caleb and Aunt Rachel and their children are just people. They are human beings same as we are. They're family."

Tildy set her jaw in the stubborn way she had when she refused to be budged from her position. She knew that the expression on her face spoke more clearly than words.

"Papa would want you to be fair, you know," Mother said gently. "You shouldn't make up your mind about persons until you really get to know them."

Tildy unclenched her teeth a bit. She knew what her mother said was true. Papa had always been a fair man.

"I know you'll love your Aunt Rachel," Mother continued. "She is so sweet and kind . . . and so pretty. Rachel always was the beauty of the family."

Suddenly Tildy felt ashamed of herself. She had been so wrapped up in her own sorrow that she had forgotten how terrible her mother must be feeling. To keep arguing with Mother at a time like this was not the way Papa would have expected his brave Matilda to act. Tildy ran across the room and threw her arms around her mother and hugged her.

"I'm sorry, Mother," Tildy said. "Nobody could be any sweeter or kinder than you are. And, I remember that Papa always said *you* were the prettiest girl he had ever seen."

It was then that their tears had started to flow that night as though they could never be stopped. The two of them, mother and daughter, stood clinging to each other in the enclosing darkness of that summer's evening as they shared the heavy grief that had come to them over the thin telegraph wire from some unknown place in Georgia.

Mother must have written the letter to her sister Rachel in Surrattsville, Maryland late that night after Tildy had finally gone up to her own bed in the loft. Tildy had found the letter on the table when she came down to breakfast the next morning.

"I think it's best," Mother had said when Tildy picked up the envelope addressed to Mrs. Caleb Larrabie in Surrattsville.

Tildy knew from the dark and heavy look around her mother's eyes that she had been unable to sleep that past night. Tildy understood because she, herself, had lain awake in the terrible stillness that had settled over the Graham house. She had felt the hours drag over her tired brain as she tried not to think how it must have been with Papa at Kennesaw Mountain.

Tildy had forced herself, instead, to remember Papa as he used to be when he was here with them whistling about his work. He had taught himself to imitate several

16

bird calls. His favorite was the thrush. Each morning when she heard him piping the melodic notes, she knew it was time for her to get out of bed. How surprised and pleased he had been when she learned that call and returned his whistle. It became a signal they exchanged. It meant, "I need your help," or "Where are you?" or "Papa's home, put dinner on."

How she missed that whistle after he went off to the army, just as she missed so many other things. She missed holding onto his big work-scarred hands that were so strong on the plow handle, but so gentle as he tucked the covers around his three daughters when they went to bed at night.

The morning after the word of Papa's death had come through, Tildy had seen the letter Mother had written to Aunt Rachel. Tildy turned the envelope face down on the table so that she wouldn't have to see the despised Maryland address. Tildy set her mind to figuring out how she would be able to keep the farm going—knowing that Papa would never be back.

"Just promise me one thing," Tildy had pleaded with her mother that day. "Please don't send this letter to Aunt Rachel right away. Give me a chance to see if I can manage the farming."

"We'll help," Elizabeth said and little Louisa had lisped that she would help, too.

Tildy saw her mother's hands knot into tight fists before she thrust them deep into her apron pockets.

"I've got to do what I think is right for all of us," Mother had said. "I've got your two sisters to consider as well."

Tildy looked across the table at Elizabeth and Louisa, both of them still in their long white nightdresses and rubbing the sleep from their eyes.

Tildy thought that Elizabeth was a lot like Mother. Her hair was the pale gold of winter wheat when the June sun highlights it. Her blue eyes were so large they gave her the expression of a fragile porcelain doll. That was probably why all the ladies at church made over her so much that Mother and Papa worried about her becoming spoiled by it all. Elizabeth was fair-skinned, like Mother was and didn't dare go out into the sun without a bonnet. She was small-boned and a bit on the thin side. Papa had often remarked that both Mother and Elizabeth could stand a bit more flesh on their bones. As much as Tildy loved her sister Elizabeth, she couldn't help wishing that she had been made of hardier stuff. Yes, it would have been better if Elizabeth had been a husky brother.

Louisa, on the other hand, was like Papa and Tildy. Sometimes when Tildy looked at the sturdy arms and legs of the little three-year-old she felt as though she were looking at a small reflection of herself. Louisa had thick, dark hair with a bit of stubborn curl that made it resist any attempt at neat braids. Both girls had the same gray eyes that sometimes looked soft as a pigeon's wing, but at other times could go steely gray as a thunderhead, depending upon their mood. Louisa, like Tildy, had a complexion that soaked in the sun and roasted to an olive shade on square hands and determined jaw. But stocky little Louisa, no matter how hard she tried, wasn't going to be much help for several more years. And help

. . . lots of help, was what Tildy knew she needed right now.

"Please, Mother, give me a chance to run the farm," Tildy begged with much more self-confidence in her voice than she was feeling inside.

Mother didn't speak for a while, then slowly nodded her head. "I suppose a little while longer won't make much difference."

Mother turned back to the stove and bent to look into the oven. But, before Mother had turned away, Tildy saw the tears that had beaded up in her mother's eyes.

As soon as Tildy finished breakfast she said to her sisters, "You girls hurry up and finish eating. Then get dressed and start looking for yard eggs."

Under her breath, Tildy prayed, "Please make me strong and brave like Queen Matilda."

2

"Mother! Mother!" Elizabeth screamed as she ran toward the house. Her blue calico dress whipped around her thin legs, making her stumble. "Come, help us, Mother! Old Maud fell down on the ground and Tildy's crying."

Just outside the barn door, Tildy was on her knees, her arms wrapped around Old Maud's neck. The horse lay on its side, its rib cage heaving and its withers shuddering. The animal's eyes were rolled back so that the whites showed.

Tildy looked up and saw that her mother's face was white, and she held her left hand across her mouth as she ran toward the barn.

"Tildy, what happened?" Her mother cried out. "Did you fall off of Maud? Are you hurt?"

Tildy shook her head because she couldn't talk with the sobs catching in her throat. She hadn't let herself cry since they had gotten the news of Papa's death a month ago.

She had not cried with disappointment when the relentless sun had finally caused the pole beans to sizzle on their vines rather than in the cooking pot as they should have done. She and her mother and two sisters had spent days lugging water in buckets up from the creek. It seemed that no matter how much water they carried, the parched earth had absorbed it as soon as

they poured it on. None of their efforts had been enough. The beans were gone, but no matter how badly her back ached from that effort, she refused to cry.

Tildy had not allowed herself to cry with frustration when the hoped-for rain finally did arrive . . . too late and too much. The Graham's corn, which had been waist high on the Fourth of July, lay beaten to the ground after the violent storm that pelted the fields with hail and washed the soil away from the roots.

Tildy had refused to let herself cry with fear that awful night when she had waited out by the barn with Papa's old shotgun across her knees. As she waited her eyes had strained to see in the dark what it was that had been getting the chickens. She had not even allowed herself much more than a triumphant grimmace when she knew she had gotten rid of that thieving fox forever.

Tildy was relieved that their egg supply had been made safe as new problems took the place of each old one. She had set her stubborn jaw once more to keep the tears from flowing when she discovered that weevils had infested the Graham's newly-ground flour. They would need that flour if they were to get through the winter ahead.

Tildy had allowed none of these things to weaken her determination to keep the farm going. She just had to prove to her mother that there was no reason to mail that letter to Aunt Rachel Larrabie saying that they would accept her invitation to move to Maryland.

But today . . . having Old Maud break her leg seemed like the final tragedy. This was the one thing that Tildy knew she simply could not cope with.

Now, Tildy crumpled to the ground and let her salty tears mingle with the sweat that glistened on the old horse's neck. She loved this dear old mare. Maud was more than just a work animal. She was a friend . . . a part of the family.

Tildy had learned to ride on Maud's broad back. Gentle Maud had moved carefully as though she knew that Tildy's small legs were not long enough to get a secure grip. Old Maud had not seemed to mind a bit when Tildy's fingers entangled themselves in the flowing chestnut mane. Maud had also carried Elizabeth and later little Louisa perched behind Tildy. She hadn't seemed to mind the added weight or the shrill laughter of the three sisters as she plodded around the barn lot.

It had been just a little over a year ago that Maud had been so patient as Papa showed a struggling Tildy how to plow a straight furrow. The animal seemed to have a sixth sense about how slow or how fast to move along the rows with Tildy holding the lines.

But Maud was old and was subject to the same arthritic pains in her aging joints that humans experience. Tildy had noticed the horse seemed to be moving more slowly lately. Then, that morning Tildy had known even before Maud fell that the terrible dry stick crack she heard was a bone breaking. That sound was like the signal to the end of everything that Tildy had worked so hard to save.

"You know what has to be done, Tildy," her mother said quietly, putting her hand on Tildy's shaking shoulder. "Do you want me to go over to the Pettibone's and have one of their boys come here and . . . ?" Mother paused as though she could not bear to say the final words out loud.

"No," Tildy shouted. The thought of having to put Maud out of her misery was bad enough, but the idea of having one of those Pettibones do it was more than she could bear.

Simon Pettibone had the biggest spread in all of Lipton County, but it wasn't enough for him. His greedy eyes had been focused on the Graham farm even before Papa marched off in his blue uniform. To ask one of the Pettibones to come over to do what must be done was like inviting them to a funeral of all the hopes and dreams that Tildy and Papa had for the farm.

"It isn't fair," Tildy moaned, hugging Maud's neck all the tighter.

Mother knelt and put her arms around Tildy. "Of course it isn't fair," Mother whispered softly.

"I worked so hard," Tildy sobbed.

"Nobody could have worked or tried any harder than you did. I am so proud of you, and Papa would be, too."

"We can't do without a horse and I don't know how to get enough money for us to buy another one," Tildy said. "I promised Papa I would run the farm, but I've failed."

"The only failures are those persons who don't even try," Mother said. "You did the best you could, Tildy. Sometimes that is all that anybody can do."

Mother's words were an echo of Papa's. It was what he always used to say.

Mother reached into her apron pocket and handed Tildy a handkerchief. Then she said firmly, "Tildy, we cannot let Maud suffer any longer."

Tildy got to her feet, still sniffling. She wiped her hand across her eyes and blew her nose.

"Elizabeth," Tildy said. "You take Louisa back to the house. You stay there until I say it's all right for you to come outside again. You hear me?" Then she turned to Mother. "I'll do what has to be done."

"You know you'll have to have some help to bury Maud when it's over," Mother insisted. "There is no way that the two of us can possibly do it."

Tildy clenched her teeth stubbornly. "I'll find somebody. If I have to walk five miles to town I'll find somebody, but I won't have help from the Pettibones. I don't want any of them stepping foot on this place."

But in the end, the Pettibones not only set foot on the Graham place. They bought it out, lock, stock, and barrel. Mr. Pettibone and his four strapping sons, none of whom had ever felt the pull of Union blue fabric across their husky shoulders, took possession of the land and the livestock and the farmhouse. They got their hands on all of the outbuildings for hardly more than Jeremiah and Rebecca Graham had paid for the acreage alone when they signed the deed six years ago.

Tildy, herself, had walked all the way to Vinsontown to mail the letter that Mother had written to Aunt Rachel in Maryland. Then, she had gone tight-lipped about the business of helping the family get ready to leave the farm and the state of Indiana.

The next several days were filled with hard choices. Choices about what they could take with them and what they would have to leave behind.

Sometimes Tildy wished she were little Louisa's age again. As long as Louisa had her homemade rag doll

Charlotte, she was happy. She didn't seem to care about anything else.

Elizabeth, too, seemed undisturbed about the move. In fact, when Mother had told her about her Maryland cousins Annabelle and Roseanne who were almost her same age, Elizabeth decided it was going to be a wonderful idea for them to move to Maryland. Elizabeth followed Mother about the house asking questions that Mother answered in the most glowing terms. Tildy couldn't help but suspect that Mother was trying to buoy up her own spirits by making Maryland sound like the most glorious place this side of heaven.

As for Tildy, there wasn't much problem about which of her possessions to take to Maryland. The only thing she really cared about was the farm. And, there was no way that she could take that with her.

Tildy knew it must have been hardest of all for Mother. There was the walnut sewing stand that Papa had made for her and the cane-bottom rocking chair. Mother could not possibly leave such things as those behind. But, there was also the little pump organ that Mother had brought with her from Pennsylvania as a bride. There were the large pictures over the mantle with the heavily carved frames, the pictures of Mother's parents. They were the grandparents that Tildy and her sisters had never seen but had heard so much about. There were the beautiful hand-pieced quilts that Mother had labored over in the evening after her day's work was done. She had put in thousands of neat, tiny stitches, straining her eyes in the flickering lamplight. Tildy knew that all of these treasures were an important part of

Mother's life. Tildy watched as Mother sorted through these bulky items. They would not be easy to pack and they would be expensive to send on the train. Tildy noticed that Mother seemed to sigh a lot as she put things in one pile or another as she tried to make her decisions.

Tildy was also painfully aware of how cautiously Mother was guarding the small amount of money that they had received from the Pettibones when they bought the Graham farm. The Grahams might be going to live with Mother's sister and family in Maryland, but Tildy knew that her mother was determined that they should pay their own expenses as much as possible. Mother said she would never let them become totally dependent on someone's charity . . . even if the Grahams and Larrabies were kinfolks.

Mother had made it clear in that letter that she would expect to earn their room and board by helping Aunt Rachel. Aunt Rachel wasn't well as she awaited the birth of her new baby.

Tildy also knew that her mother planned to do some sewing for the people of Surrattsville where Aunt Rachel and Uncle Caleb lived. Tildy had no doubt that as soon as the people there saw the beautiful handwork that Mother did, they would be more than glad to pay her to make clothing for them. Tildy was aware that, in her own fashion, Mother was as determined as she was to do things her own way.

Reverend Martin and the women of the Christian Church were very helpful when the word got around that the Grahams were packing up to leave. They brought in food so that Mother would not have to cook meals when she had so many other things to do. In a way, such kindness made Tildy sad, for it reminded her of the way the women had helped when Papa died.

It made Tildy feel somewhat better that it was Reverend Martin who had purchased the desk that Papa had made.

"If you find that you have room for this in Maryland, you write and tell me," Reverend Martin had said. "I will find a way to get it to you there."

Tildy saw Mother bite her lip to keep the tears back. "That's ever so kind of you," she said.

"Otherwise," Reverend Martin promised, "I'll take good care of it until you come back to Indiana someday. Then, the desk shall be yours once more."

At that Tildy herself had a hard time trying to keep back the tears. She knew that the thought of ever returning to Indiana was the most impossible of dreams, but she couldn't help but grasp at the thought. It was a touchstone of hope. She clutched at it even as she clutched A Child's History of England, the little book that Papa had read to her.

Leaving the farm had been made even harder because of the Pettibones. Old Mr. Pettibone and his two oldest sons, Buck and Mabry, had not even been able to wait until the Grahams had gone before they came over. They swaggered possessively around the Graham property. The worst thing for Tildy had been watching the Pettibones paint that big, gray, five-pointed star on the barn door. That star was just like the one the Pettibones had painted on their own barn door. Tildy was enraged by their putting their mark on the barn that Papa had built. She wanted to rush outside and insist that they stop what they were doing. Mother must have sensed what was going on in Tildy's mind as she saw her start out the back door of the house.

"Tildy," her mother said firmly, "Sometimes it's wise to know when to keep silent."

Tildy stood at the screen door thinking that if she could find a can of paint, she'd paint over that star as soon as the Pettibones left.

The Pettibones had seen her watching from the doorway and they had laughed out loud as Mabry called out in his rough voice, "Don't let the Nu-Oh-Lac's get you."

Tildy had moved back inside the house where they couldn't see her. She wondered what kind of a crazy thing that was for them to say to her. And as she turned she saw her Mother standing behind her, white-faced and with a strange expression on her face. Tildy started to ask what was wrong, but somehow realized that Mother did not want to talk about what was happening, nor did she want to have to discuss the matter with Tildy.

Tildy couldn't understand why this whole thing made her feel so shivery inside. If only Papa were here, she wouldn't have to be frightened.

3

Reverend Martin took the Grahams to Indianapolis in his wagon. As he helped them board the train at the station, Tildy needed all her courage. Having him around to help them reminded her how much the family needed a man. It reminded her even more how much they needed Papa. It reminded her of how far away they were going from the farm where they had all been together. When Reverend Martin put out his hand to shake hers, Tildy threw both of her arms about him and hugged him tightly as though she simply could not bear to let him go.

"The train will be leaving soon," Mother said in a very soft voice, and Tildy wondered if she were feeling much the same way.

Tildy let Reverend Martin go, but she watched him from the window and waved until she could not see him any longer.

As she finally settled back in her seat she couldn't help but think that the rhythmic sound of the great wheels on the track were like some giant monster gobbling up the countryside she loved so much. Tildy peered out of the window with a hunger in her heart that was more intense than any emptiness of her stomach had ever been. Even when noontime came and Mother spread out the contents of the wicker basket that the church women had packed, Tildy could not bring herself to look away from the moving scene outside.

"Fried chicken, Tildy." Her mother tried to tempt her.

"And gingerbread," Louisa added, wide-eyed with anticipation.

"And peach preserves for the biscuits," Elizabeth said. "Your favorite."

But even peach preserves weren't as important to Tildy right now as it was for her to fill her mind with an indelible picture of Indiana. She did not know when, if ever, she would see it again.

She wanted to be certain never to forget the look of the white-trunked sycamores with three different kinds of leaves on each tree. She tried to memorize the way the old split rail fences zig-zagged along the side of the honey-gold fields. Here and there, in the timothy, like a flaming candle, were the red spikes of the cardinal flower. Once Tildy caught sight of a great blue heron standing patiently in the waters of a stream, its rapier like bill ready to spear an unsuspecting fish. Each sight was like a chain reaction, setting off in her mind some memory that was a deep ache—like the milkweed seeds that she knew were now popping open, their scimitar-shaped pods split open to reveal hair as silky white as that on the top of Reverend Martin's head.

Tildy recalled the year she had painstakingly gathered the milkweed fiber, as it burst from the leathery pods. She had then carefully picked from it the clinging little black seeds. Finally, she had enough to use to stuff a small pillow ticking that she had stitched for Papa. She had given it to him for Christmas. How he had praised its down softness. "More comfortable than any goose or duck feather pillow I ever had."

As the train huffed toward the Ohio border, Tildy saw stretches of the old Whitewater Canal.

"Your Papa and I traveled part of the way on a canal boat when we came west from Pennsylvania," Mother said, and Tildy was certain she detected a wistful tone in her mother's voice. "Now it's gone, like so many things."

Mother had spoken so softly that Tildy wasn't sure Mother had actually been speaking to her. Tildy looked at her mother and saw the tears hovering in the corners of her eyes. Tildy knew she wasn't the only one who was having to leave a place where the memories had deep roots.

As the train crossed over the border into Ohio and left Indiana behind, everything seemed changed. Tildy knew full well that the land and the trees and the fields and the entire look of the place were practically the same, but in her heart-of-hearts she felt herself in a strange land. Nothing on this side of the state line meant anything to her. She slumped back wearily in her seat and was able to turn at last from the window.

Louisa held out a piece of gingerbread and said, "It's the very last piece, Tildy. I wanted to eat it, but we saved it for you."

Tildy took the treasure from her sister's small, chubby hand. She broke it in three pieces, giving the other two to Louisa and Elizabeth. Tildy ate the spicy cake slowly, savoring it as though it were the last vestige of Indiana.

It was late afternoon by the time the train pulled into the station at Cincinnati. They felt lucky to locate a boardinghouse within a few blocks' walking distance of the depot. After a light supper they went upstairs to their room to bed.

Tildy stood at the small bedroom window and looked out at what little she could see of this great city. She remembered that Papa once had told her that Cincinnati was called the "Athens of the West." She wished she could go for a walk to see some of this grand place, but she was more tired from the long day on the train than if she had been hoeing corn rows from sunup to sunset.

Even little Louisa did not whine to stay up "just a little bit longer," when Mother got the nightgowns from the carpetbags.

"We've got to be up early if we're to have a good breakfast and then be back at the train station to catch the 6:30 train in the morning."

The next day, as the train clacked its way across the broad state of Ohio, Tildy discovered she had an entirely different feeling about their journey. Yesterday, she had wanted the train to slow down so that she could capture every sight of Indiana before it slipped from her grasp. Today, however, she was anxious for the long trip to end.

Tildy was tired of being cooped up in the box-like contraption that was the train. She was tired of the hard, uncomfortable seats. She was weary of trying to think of things to do to amuse her younger sisters.

"Tildy, play Cat's Cradle with me," Elizabeth begged.

"But Elizabeth, we've already played that game at least twenty times today," Tildy sighed.

Elizabeth held out the piece of string, which was no longer white, and looked at Tildy with her wide blue eyes.

As Tildy started to take the piece of string to start the old game again, Louisa pushed it away. "No, don't do that," the little girl whined. "Tell me a story."

"Here," Mother said, pulling Louisa up onto her lap. "I'll tell a story while Tildy and Elizabeth play Cat's Cradle."

By the time the train reached Bepre late in the day, Tildy felt like a limp rag. Elizabeth had finally tired of the string games and had put her head in Tildy's lap. She had been asleep for over an hour now. Tildy was grateful for that, but her arms ached from the effort of trying to hold Elizabeth's head in a comfortable position as the train bumped along.

Louisa slept, too, while Tildy and her mother both rode silently, each busy with her own thoughts.

The train slowed as it approached the station, lurching as it halted. It threw them forward and then back into the seats. The two young girls slept on.

"Wake up, Elizabeth. You've got to help carry the picnic basket," Tildy urged. "I have to get our bags."

Tildy lifted her sister's drowsy head from her lap and tried to smooth out her skirt, which had twisted up and wrinkled badly.

Louisa stirred as Mother started to rise from the seat and disturbed her slumber.

"Look Louisa," Mother said. "The train has stopped and we are going to get on a ferry boat and cross the Ohio River. Get down and walk so I can help Tildy with the bags."

Louisa, still sleepy, put her small arms around Mother's neck tightly. Despite coaxing from both Mother and

Tildy, the little girl refused to get down and walk on her own. So, the overloaded little family struggled awkwardly off the train.

That night was much like the last. They managed to find lodgings, but the rooming house was a few more blocks farther walk than they had to go the night before. It hadn't been easy making their way along the sidewalks. Elizabeth complained about how tired she was and how heavy the picnic basket was. Tildy continually dropped things as she tried to balance twice her usual load of bags. Mother had to stop continually to loosen Louisa's stranglehold on her neck. They were all in quite bad humor when they arrived at their destination.

Tildy had a difficult time stifling her disappointment at their room. She would have preferred having the large front bedroom on the first floor—the one with the pleasant bay window that she had seen as they approached the large frame house with the sign, ROOMS TO LET. She sighed audibly, however, as they labored up several flights of stairs to a cramped and musty attic room. Tildy was sure Mother had chosen this one to try to conserve their funds. The one window in this room was so high and tiny that Tildy could not see anything but rooftops. She mourned that there was no opportunity to see any of the sights in the places where they stayed. She made a silent vow that someday she would come back and take a good long look at them.

The next morning seemed to be part of an extended nightmare. It had been dark when they awakened and hurried to get dressed, carry their luggage downstairs, and eat breakfast. They managed to get to the train station in plenty of time to catch the 6:00 train out of Parkersburg, only to discover that the train was late.

Tildy felt like crying as she realized that they could have stayed in bed longer. They were all so tired, they could have used their sleep in a bed rather than sitting on a hard bench in a railroad station waiting room. Louisa climbed up on Mother's lap and Elizabeth stretched out on the bench with her head on Tildy's lap. Tildy envied the little girls, who were able to sleep while the Grahams waited for the overdue train.

When the engine finally did pull into the station, it was a struggle to arouse the sleepy younger children and get them and all their luggage up the train steps. Because the train had been late, it pulled away almost immediately, which made it no easy task to try to get all their luggage stowed away as the train swayed and rumbled along. The lateness of the Parkersburg train meant that they almost missed their connections at Grafton. So, once again, they had to scurry about getting children and luggage off one train and onto another. Their energy and patience were wearing very thin by this time, but there was to be no relief for them. When they finally managed to get aboard the train for Washington Junction, they discovered that there were no seats available for them.

"The closer a person gets to Washington City, the more crowded the trains are," said a kind woman who offered to hold Louisa on her lap.

Tildy looked about the train coach. People were squeezed into every available inch of room on the seats. Many passengers stood in the aisles or sat on their trunks. Only two men in the railroad car were seated.

They were both wearing the blue uniforms of the Union army. One of those men had his pant leg turned up at the knee and Tildy looked away quickly. The other man— actually a young boy who couldn't have been more than sixteen years of age, had his head wrapped in bandages. He had one arm in a sling. His face was almost as white as the bandages he wore.

Tildy noticed her mother's hand go up to her mouth in a quick motion to hide the moan that escaped her lips.

"My name is Mrs. Duffy," said the woman who held Louisa on her lap. "I'm on my way to Washington to try to find my son. He was in a hospital there once before when he was wounded the first time. That was right after Manassas in sixty-one."

The woman loosened the drawstring on her little hand crocheted reticule and dug about in the little pouch.

"This came for me only yesterday," Mrs. Duffy said, holding up a piece of paper. Tildy took a deep breath when she saw it. It reminded her too much of the paper that Mr. Scroggins had handed to Mother the night he and Reverend Martin had come to their door to tell them about Papa.

"This paper says that he was wounded again. He was in a skirmish at Petersburg, Virginia."

Tildy turned her eyes toward her feet and concentrated on the sound of the train. She tried not to listen to the well-meaning woman. She did not want to hear any more about war and battles and wounded soldiers. It reminded her too much of Papa who was never coming back to them. But, even turning her head away or trying to think of something else could not shut out the sound of the woman's voice or close off the sight of the blue uniforms all about her. Tildy squeezed her eyes shut tightly and swayed slightly with the motion of the train.

"Little lady, are you ill?" someone asked, putting a hand on Tildy's arm to steady her. "Someone give her a seat before she swoons."

The soldier with the turned-up pant leg struggled on his cane to rise.

"Oh, no," Tildy insisted. "I'm all right. I'm just tired and it is too hot in here."

"Stand back from her a bit," Mrs. Duffy said as she dug about in her reticule once more. Mrs. Duffy took out a clean handkerchief and sprinkled a bit of cologne on it and handed it to Tildy.

"Here, child," Mrs. Duffy said. "Put this under your nose if you feel faint. It will revive you."

She knew Mrs. Duffy meant well, but Tildy was embarrassed at all the attention that was directed toward her. After all, Tildy did not consider herself some silly, fainting female one read about in books. And, she didn't like having everyone stare at her.

Tildy was thankful when the three-hour train ride was over and she stepped out onto the wooden platform at Washington Junction. She was terribly disappointed, however, to learn that they would have to wait until the next morning in order to get on another train, which would take them the last thirty-one miles to Washington City.

"I know of a reputable boardinghouse," Mrs. Duffy said, puffing as she walked over to them. "The woman who owns the place is a decent sort and she always puts fresh bed linens out for her guests."

Tildy gulped. During the entire trip it had never occurred to her that in the other places where they had spent the night it was possible that they might have been sleeping between bedclothes that had been used by other travelers before them. Mother was always so particular about clean covers at home. Mother would boil the linens and scrub them in lye soap and hang them in the sunshine to bleach as they dried.

Right now, Tildy wanted more than anything for this terrible trip to be over and done with. Maryland was actually beginning to seem better and better the more she thought about it. Once they reached Aunt Rachel's house, they would be able to stay put and not drag about from pillar to post. And, Tildy was certain that if Aunt Rachel was anything at all like Mother, the bed linens and the house would be spotlessly clean.

The rooms at the boardinghouse that had been recommended to them by Mrs. Duffy were a bit more expensive than those they had occupied in other places. Tildy could sense that her mother was quickly calculating what this would do to her carefully thought out budget.

Tildy moved close to Mother's ear and looked pleadingly at her as she whispered, "Clean bed linens."

Mother swallowed hard and then nodded in agreement and paid out the money.

As they were climbing the stairs to their room, Mother said, "I think we would all rest better tonight if we had baths."

"Hot baths are extra," said the boardinghouse woman.

Tildy supposed that by this time Mother had thrown caution to the winds because she said, "So be it. We cannot arrive at the Larrabie's looking like nomads."

That evening, even though she was exhausted from the long, uncomfortable day, Tildy could not fall asleep right after dinner and her bath. She lay awake in the bed that she shared with Elizabeth. She wondered about Maryland and what their life would be like there. If only Papa were with them perhaps it wouldn't be so bad. She felt a tear run out of the corner of her eye and down her cheek onto the starched white pillowcase.

Papa always used to say, "You can manage anything you have to do if you just put your mind to it."

In a way, she guessed that Papa would always be with her as long as she could remember so clearly the things that he had told her. In the darkness she could remember exactly how his voice sounded. She knew that she would never forget that.

The next morning after breakfast, the Grahams started out for the station. Tildy said a silent prayer of thanks that this would be their last day on the road. Mrs. Duffy, the nice woman from the train, led the way. The woman kept making little clucking noises to keep them all together. Tildy couldn't help but smile to herself as she imagined what they must look like. In her mind's eye, Tildy could picture her little bantam hen herding her unruly chicks about the barnyard back in Indiana.

The train to Washington was late. Mrs. Duffy assured them that was usual. When it finally arrived and they boarded, they found that it was even more crowded than the cars had been the day before. Mrs. Duffy said that was nothing out of the ordinary either.

Tildy noticed that everyone boarding the train looked tired or worried or sad or impatient or a combination of all four. People pushed and shoved together like cattle. There was no friendly visiting. Tildy was surprised to observe that few of the men on this coach paid any attention to the many women and children who stood in the crowded aisles while they sat.

The Grahams had to stand. Mother and Tildy kept a tight hold on Elizabeth and Louisa as the train thumped along over the uneven tracks. Several times they all nearly lost their balance as the train shuddered to an unexpected stop.

"They've let these tracks go to wrack and ruin since the war started," someone complained loudly.

What should have been a journey of a little over an hour took almost three hours, and by the time the train pulled into the station, it was after mid-day.

Washington City was not at all what Tildy had expected the nation's capital to be. Run-down shacks lined the streets and there were even tents pitched on the grounds in front of the President's house. On almost every corner there was a tavern and in between there were livery stables. In front of the large hotels, black men waited, asking whoever passed if they might carry their packages. They sought any kind of work at all that they might do in order to earn some money.

The late summer heat closed over the Grahams like a wet wool blanket. Tildy found herself gasping for breath as they picked their way through the dusty streets. The

41

thoroughfares seemed to Tildy more like barn lots rather than grand avenues. They were full of squawking chickens, rooting pigs, and argumentative ducks.

Louisa cried that the mosquitoes were eating her alive and slapped at them frantically as though she were doing some strange dance.

Mother was embarrassed and had to scold Elizabeth when the little girl cried out, "Mother, that man in the fine clothes who just passed by us had scented whiskers. I could *smell* them."

Washington City was certainly more crowded than any place Tildy had ever seen before. People rushed along the streets in every direction. In fact, everyone seemed to be in a great hurry. There was a scramble of carriages and horse-drawn rail cars as well as long lines of army wagons and artillery caissons rumbling along. On one occasion, the Graham family had to wait while cattle were herded across the thoroughfare.

"Put your handkerchief over your mouth," Mother instructed the girls as brown clouds of dust swirled about them.

Even after the cattle had passed by, Tildy left her handkerchief up over her nose because of the swampy smell that hung over the place. That aroma mingled with the stench of wood smoke, all of which created an evil vapor.

The man at the livery stable went about his work as though the Grahams were a minor annoyance. They had to follow him about as they tried to make arrangements with him.

"I can rent you a nice little buggy for the trip to Surrattsville today. Then, as soon as I can I'll send a stable boy in a wagon with your belongings from the train station. The wagon will be an extra four dollars."

Once again Tildy could tell by her mother's tight lips that she was wondering how she could afford that as well as what it would cost them to store the crates containing their household goods until the wagon picked them up.

"How long do you think we would have to wait for a wagon?" Mother asked the man.

"Oh, I've got the wagon right now. I just don't have a boy to drive it. These are busy times and finding help isn't easy."

Tildy said to her mother, "There's no need for us to have to rent both a buggy and a wagon to get us to Aunt Rachel's. Why can't we all ride in the wagon along with our household goods from the train station? I could drive the wagon myself and we can leave right now."

That suggestion stopped the liveryman in his work. He turned and pushed his hat back on his forehead with a gesture that plainly indicated disbelief at what he was hearing.

"Well now, missy. That seems like a mighty big undertaking for a little gal your size."

Tildy ignored the scoffing man and pleaded with her mother, "You know that Papa always let me drive our wagon back home. I'm sure I can do it."

Mother hesitated for only a moment before she said to the liveryman, "My daughter is right. She can handle horses better than most boys I know."

So it was that Tildy climbed up onto the seat of the wagon. Mother and Elizabeth and Louisa sat beside her. Tildy took a deep breath and said a prayer that she had not overestimated her own ability just because she was angry at the livery stable man. She wrapped the lines about her hands for a firm grasp, braced herself, and snapped the lines sharply. The wagon jerked forward and it was all she could do to manage the horses, but she held on tightly to let them know who was in charge.

After collecting their crates at the railroad station and asking directions to Surrattsville, Tildy headed the wagon out along 11th Street toward the Navy Yard Bridge over the Potomac River.

Tildy couldn't help but notice that almost everyone they passed looked at them with eyes blinking in amazement. Tildy sat up very straight and proud, determined not to let any of that bother her. What she did not anticipate, however, was how their unusual arrival would affect Uncle Caleb Larrabie.

4

It soon became clear to Tildy that the arrival of the Graham family and their household goods in Surrattsville, Maryland was something of a rude shock to the Larrabies.

It wasn't that Tildy with her mother and her two sisters were not expected by the Larrabies. It was their mode of transportation that created such a great stir in the entire neighborhood. Uncle Caleb Larrabie let it be known in no uncertain terms that he didn't approve of it at all.

By the time the wagon loaded with all the Graham possessions and family members had rumbled along New Cut Road and past the Surratt Tavern and entered the cross road, they had become the leader of a strange and noisy parade.

The wagon itself rattled and squeeked along as the springs groaned over every rut and hole in the road. Behind them trailed a crowd of hooting boys and barking dogs.

"Whoa," Tildy called, pulling up firmly on the reins. She turned to the children in the road. "Can anyone of you tell me where Caleb Larrabie's place is?"

Not one of the boys following the wagon answered. They simply looked at each other and laughed without answering her.

Tildy repeated her question but still received no reply. Irritated at their unhelpfulness, she shouted at them, "The Larrabie place. Where is the Larrabie place?"

At last one of the boys shouted something back at her. Tildy stood up with her hands on her hips looking at the children who were milling about the wagon. She wondered what in the world could be the language they spoke. She found that she could not understand any of their drawled words. And, it occurred to her that if she could not understand them, they might be having as much difficulty understanding her.

Very slowly she pronounced the word, "Larrabie."

One small boy squinted up at her and pointed a grubby finger to the west. Tildy looked in that direction and saw a large, two-story, clapboard house. She cracked the lines and once more the wagon bumped forward slowly.

When they reached the side road, she pulled hard to the left and shouted, "Haw," and the horses obediently turned. The loaded wagon leaned and Elizabeth and Louisa squeeled and clutched at Mother. The wagon continued its progress, still followed by the hollering, hooting crowd.

"Whoa now," Tildy shouted again and drew up hard on the lines. The horses halted at her command in front of the sizable house that the boy had pointed out to Tildy.

Tildy breathed a huge sigh of relief and looked about her. The first person she saw was a tall, buxom black woman who was standing on the porch of the house.

The woman carried a small blond-haired child on one of her broad hips. It seemed to Tildy that the woman grabbed the little boy tighter when the loaded wagon came to a stop in front of the house. Then Tildy noticed that there were three other small, blond boys crowding so close to the woman they were almost hidden in the folds of her long, full skirt.

"You all stay right here by me till we find out what this here commotion's all about," the black woman instructed them.

It was then that Tildy noticed another woman. This one was as pale and fair as the first woman was dark. The pale woman was not out on the porch of the house. She stood inside at one of the tall front windows. This second woman had pulled back the lace curtains to peek outside. Beside the pale woman were the equally pale faces of two young girls.

By this time, the Larrabie place seemed to come alive with people. From around the back of the house came a tall, gaunt man with a sallow complexion. He was followed by a lanky boy who was a younger version of the man, with the same yellowish complexion. Behind them was a stockily-built young black boy who Tildy guessed was about her own age. Peeking around the opposite corner of the house was a young black woman.

"What's all the ruckus out here, Juno?" the sour-faced man said to the black woman standing on the front porch of the house.

The woman, still clutching the child, shrugged her shoulders and shook her head. "Don't know as I can say."

47

"Are you Caleb Larrabie?" Tildy called as she clambered down from the wagon seat to the ground.

"I might be," the man said, squinting his eyes as he stared back at her. "Who wants to know?"

At that moment the front door of the house opened. The pale woman who had been watching from the window hurried outside as fast as her bulky body would allow her to move.

"Becky. Becky," the pale woman called, holding out her arms. "Is it really you, at last?"

Tildy and Elizabeth and Louisa watched as their mother quickly got down from her seat on the wagon and, holding her skirts, ran to the pale woman. The two of them hugged each other. Both of them were half-laughing and half-crying all at the same time.

"My dear, dear sister Rachel," Mother said, tears glistening on her tired face. "How good it is to see you after so long a time."

"It has been a very long time, Rebecca," Aunt Rachel said. "You cannot imagine how much I have missed you these many years."

The man moved forward unsmiling. His voice was rough as he said, "Continue this reunion inside the house like respectable folks. I think there has been quite enough of this show for the entertainment of our neighbors."

Aunt Rachel drew back as though she had touched a hot stove. Her white face showed color for the first time. "How very thoughtless of me," she said. "You all must be tired from your travels. Do come inside. We'll provide you with some refreshment."

Tildy lifted Elizabeth and Louisa down from the wagon seat. The three Graham girls followed Mother and Aunt Rachel into the Larrabie house.

As Uncle Caleb and his gawky son returned to whatever it was they were doing out back, Tildy heard him complaining, with no apparent attempt to lower his voice, "Well, it seems our kinfolks have treated the people of Surrattsville to an unseemly spectacle they'll be chewing on for days. I don't appreciate being made a laughingstock of the neighborhood."

The boy, dogging his father's heels said, "Imagine a bunch of females coming here unescorted that way driving a wagon like that."

Uncle Caleb's last words before he rounded the corner of the house were, "Juno. Show Mrs. Graham and her daughters to their room so that they can clean up and make themselves presentable."

The tall black woman nodded amiably. She was still carrying the small boy on her hip and shepherding the three others at her full skirts as she led the Grahams into the front hallway.

"We got to climb up these steps, ladies," Juno said to Mother, going ahead of her into the wide entryway.

Aunt Rachel paused at the lower landing. "Please forgive me, my dears. I cannot manage those stairs right now. I'll wait for you in the front parlor. Come down whenever you are ready and we can talk to our hearts' content then. We've got so much to catch up on."

Tildy noticed that as she stood, Aunt Rachel had to reach out and steady herself by leaning on the stair rail.

"Here Juno, let me take the boys with me until you come down. Roseanne and Annabelle can help me watch them for this little while. Come now, Edmund, Jefferson, Calhoun."

The three boys hiding in Juno's skirts fled to their mother's skirts where they could peek out in safety at the Grahams.

"Now Juno, give me Summy."

"No, ma'am," said Juno. "He's too much for you to handle right now and I'm used to him here on my hip."

"Very well," Aunt Rachel said as though she were a child being given instructions by an adult. She turned and went into the parlor with her three young sons firmly attached to her skirts.

Tildy herself was puffing as she followed Juno up the stairs. She could understand why her frail Aunt Rachel had not attempted to come with them. Tildy had supposed their rooms would be on the second floor, but they merely paused again on that landing. Juno opened a low, narrow door. Squeezing through it, Juno led them up still another flight of stairs. The steps were steep and dark. At the top they opened onto a single attic room at the top of the house. It was a large room but had a low ceiling, which made it seem rather confined.

"I reckon my boy Cato will be up soon with your belongings," Juno said. "You send your dresses back downstairs with him. I'll get the wrinkles all smoothed out by dinner time. Mr. Caleb likes for folks to be dressed up fittin' for evening meal. I'll be back directly with a basin of water for your washing-up."

"You don't have to make another trip up all those

stairs for us," Tildy said to Juno. "Elizabeth and I will go back down with you and carry the water up here for ourselves."

Juno paused for a moment and inspected Tildy closely with her coal-black eyes. "Mr. Caleb would have my hide on the barn door if I let you ladies do your own fetching and hauling."

"But you shouldn't be expected to wait on us," Tildy objected. "You've got other things to do."

Juno threw back her head and laughed as she said, "Now, you ladies just get out of those travel clothes and take a lay-down. This kind of weather can put you under. 'Specially hard on folks not used to it. I'll be back soon with your washing-up water."

Then, Juno was gone, moving surprisingly fast for such a large woman and a woman still carrying a small boy on her hip.

Tildy stood watching Juno go down the attic steps. She couldn't quite figure out what it was but Tildy knew that there was something about Juno that made her a person you didn't argue with.

Tildy and Mother turned to help Elizabeth and Louisa slip out of their dusty dresses as Juno had directed. Tildy supposed all of them did look a sight after several long days traveling. While they waited for Juno to come back with the water, Elizabeth and Louisa settled on two of the little cots in one corner of the room. Their eyes were shut almost the minute their heads touched the pillows.

Tildy sat down on the edge of her bed and inspected their new living quarters more closely. There were four narrow bedsteads that had been painted a fresh white. There was a small washstand and a tall wardrobe up against the wall on one side of the room. A tiny mirror hanging on the wall and a braided rag rug in the center completed the furnishings. It was sparse, but Tildy supposed it was all they really needed. The best part was that it was clean.

Mother was standing by the small window. "Maybe this is why your Aunt Rachel looks so peaked," Mother said, taking in a deep breath.

"What, Mother?" Tildy asked, her mind more on the unfamiliar surroundings than on that pale, shell-like woman who was her mother's sister.

"This weather," Mother said. "Perhaps it is this oppressive, damp heat that makes your Aunt Rachel seem so weak and drawn-looking." Mother turned away from the window and sat down on her own bed. "Of course, she is only a short time away from the arrival of the new baby, but I didn't like the way that she gasped for air after the slightest exertion."

Tildy thought her mother might be right and that it was just the hot, humid weather or the waiting for the new baby that was the reason for Aunt Rachel's worn-down look. Somehow though, Tildy thought it might be something else. Aunt Rachel made Tildy think of a stray dog that has been mistreated and just wants to stay out of trouble. Surely there was more to Aunt Rachel's defeated look than Mother thought.

Tildy and Mother were both glad to wash the travel grime from their faces and brush their hair and put it up neatly again. They decided to leave Elizabeth and Louisa asleep on their cots instead of taking them downstairs to the parlor where Aunt Rachel and her children waited.

As Mother and Tildy entered the room, Juno appeared and lured Edmund and the twins Jefferson and Calhoun into the kitchen with promises of shortcake and cream.

The parlor was as grand a room as Tildy had ever seen. Heavy ecru-colored curtains hung at the tall windows and fanned out onto the red-flowered carpet. Tildy thought they looked like the train of a queen's ball gown.

In one corner of the room stood a huge piano with great carved legs. Aunt Rachel said that it was made of rosewood. Tildy didn't really know what that was, but the way Aunt Rachel said it, Tildy was certain it must be something very special. On each side of the piano's scrolled music rack were lamps with crystal ornaments that caught the sunlight and reflected rainbows on the opposite walls.

Paintings in gilt frames adorned each of the four walls. On the marble mantle over the fireplace were lovely little china figurines of elaborately dressed men and women.

Everywhere she turned to look there was a new bit of wonderment for Tildy to admire. She couldn't help but think how different this place was from the simple furniture of the Graham farmhouse back in Indiana. It was almost as if a page of a storybook had been recreated here. Tildy would have liked to wander about the room examining all these beautiful things, but Aunt Rachel invited her and Mother to sit down near her. So, Tildy had to content herself with letting her fingers examine the intricately woven brocade design of the upholstery beneath her skirts. And when she thought no one was looking, she touched the gilded rosebuds that had been carved on the wooden arms of the loveseat where she sat.

Aunt Rachel settled into a cushioned chair opposite Tildy and her mother. This gave Tildy a good chance to look at Aunt Rachel. It was hard for Tildy to believe that this was her mother's sister—the one that Mother always spoke of so proudly as being the beauty of the family. Today, amid the fine surroundings of her home, Aunt Rachel looked more like a wilted rose.

Tildy turned her attention to her two cousins, Annabelle and Roseanne. The two young girls sat on small chairs, one on each side of their mother. If Aunt Rachel resembled a faded flower, her little daughters looked like blossoms in springtime. The petal-like skirts of their identical yellow dresses billowed out about them reminding Tildy of the buttercups that grew wild in the fields back home. Nine-year-old Roseanne had the same pale complexion as Aunt Rachel, but she also had honey-colored hair and bright blue eyes. Tildy thought the little girl looked enough like Elizabeth that the two cousins could be sisters. Annabelle, who was eleven years old, was the very opposite of Roseanne in appearance. Annabelle had the dark hair of her father, Caleb Larrabie. Her eyes seemed as black as though someone had drawn them in with charcoal. Each of the girls had her hair tightly curled in ringlets and both wore small lacy caps decorated with long trailing ribbons. Their tiny feet, encased in white high button shoes, barely peeped out from beneath their lace-trimmed pantaloons.

The two girls worked on bits of embroidery as they sat quietly by their mother. They entered into the conversation saying only, "Yes, ma'am," and "No, ma'am," whenever addressed directly but never venturing a comment of their own. Their demure manner made Tildy uncomfortable. For the first time in her life she felt shy and could not think of anything to say.

Tildy noticed that Aunt Rachel's fancywork lay untouched in her lap. Occasionally she raised her pink lace fan, but even the effort to stir the air with it seemed too much for her. Her hands would flutter back onto her lap like white, wounded birds.

Tildy soon grew tired of sitting and listening as Mother described the long train trip from Indiana to Maryland. Tildy didn't want to think about that ever again. It had been miserable, but it was over now. She preferred to put it out of her mind.

When she could find a pause in the adult's conversation, Tildy asked, "May I please be excused? I would like to go outside and get some fresh air."

Tildy saw her two cousins stop their stitchery to look at her and then at each other in a startled fashion. Tildy felt as though she had suggested something as outrageous as burning down the house.

"If it's all right with your mother," Aunt Rachel said. "But, you must be very careful in the mid-day heat. There are some hats hanging on the hall tree. Be certain to cover up and not take any sun."

Tildy really didn't want to have anything on her head, but decided it was best not to make an issue of it. Obediently she selected a straw hat with a wide floppy brim. She put it on and tied it securely under her chin. She peered at herself with amusement in the large mirror in the hallway. Her freckled nose gave clear evidence that she had taken plenty of sun when she worked out in the fields at home.

Tildy went out onto the porch and looked about at the Larrabie house and their fields, which lay beyond. She went down the steps and kicked the toe of her shoe into the mustard-colored dirt. It didn't seem as fertile to her as the dark, Indiana loam she knew so well. She stooped and picked up a handful of soil, crumbling it between her fingers. It seemed to Tildy that it contained a lot of clay and gravel.

Tildy sighed and stood up and walked around to the back of the house. There were the usual outbuildings found on most farms, but Tildy noticed that the barns were painted black and there were wide spaces between the siding. She wondered why they were built that way.

Beyond the barns were tall plants with broad leaves. These were plants she didn't recognize. She started to walk closer to them hoping to examine them more closely. At that moment, Juno came out the back door and saw her.

"Well, for land's sake, child. What are you doing out in this heat?"

"I like being outside," Tildy said. "It's ever so much better than being cooped up in the house. I spend most of my time outside when I am at home."

Juno shook her head and made a funny clicking sound with her tongue.

"Dinner time soon," Juno said, her heavy arms reaching up to pull the cord attached to a metal bell. As it clanged, Juno said, "You best hurry. Get yourself ready for sitting up to the table."

Reluctantly, Tildy went back inside and to the parlor. It was empty. Aunt Rachel and her cousins and her mother were no longer there. The window shades had been drawn together and the room was dark.

Tildy was tempted to take this opportunity to explore the fancy room now that she was alone. Just as she had moved over to the fireplace mantle and was about to pick up one of the little figurines, she heard a heavy footstep behind her. She whirled guiltily. It was Juno.

"I was looking for my mother," Tildy explained, wondering if Juno were twins. The woman seemed to be a presence everywhere about the house.

"All the folks are getting ready for dinner," Juno said. "I got to close these parlor doors now."

Tildy went out into the entryway hall as Juno pulled the heavy double doors together.

Aimlessly, Tildy wandered down the broad center hallway. Then she caught sight of herself in the large mirror. She saw that she was still wearing that silly hat. She took it off and tried to smooth her hair.

She stood looking at her own reflection. She saw her chin begin to pucker and her gray eyes became cloudy with tears. She wished she were at home. She wanted more than anything to be back in Indiana, back on their old farm. As she stared at the mirror, she seemed to see her father's eyes looking back at her. She knew what he would say, "Be my brave Queen Matilda."

Tildy took a deep breath and wiped her hands across her eyes. Then she turned and walked slowly toward the back of the house where the dining room was located.

All of the Larrabies and the Grahams were gathered about the long table. Uncle Caleb, from his place at the head of the table, looked up at her unsmilingly. Without saying a word he nodded toward an empty chair next to Mother. Tildy slipped into it just as silently.

Juno was serving the soup course from a large tureen. Tildy noticed that Juno's son Cato had changed from his working clothes into a short, red jacket and white pants. He stood in one corner of the room pulling a cord back and forth with a regular cadence. The cord was attached to an oversized feather fan that was suspended high above the table. The noise of the cord moving back and forth over its small pulley and the slight rustle of the fan accompanied the tinkle of silver spoons on the china soup bowls. Other than that, there were no other sounds in the room.

Tildy thought it strange to have so many people gathered around the big table and so little noise.

Back home, the evening meal had always been one of the best times of the day for the Graham family. Each person, even little Louisa, had been encouraged to share some interesting thing that had happened during the day. Tildy would tell of some incident at school. Mother would tell how she had found a new wildflower blooming. Elizabeth would be excited about finding a nest of blue robin's eggs. How they would laugh when Louisa explained that her rag dolly had been very naughty today and would not take a nap.

Papa, himself, was always a great one for talking about the events of the times. He used to say, with a bit of pride, that his one extravagance was having the newspaper from Indianapolis sent to him. He said he felt he had a responsibility to know what was going on in the world.

Dinner time at the Graham's had been a lively occasion, usually accompanied by much talk and laughter. The contrast with the way the Larrabies sat at table was a curiosity for Tildy. Here everyone seemed completely busy with eating. As she waited to be served, Tildy took the opportunity to sneak a look at Uncle Caleb. He, too, had changed from his working clothes. He wore a black frock coat and a starched white collar with a black string tie. Lucius and the other boys were each dressed in similar fashion. Tildy couldn't remember seeing another man dressed that way except for Reverend Martin when he was preaching.

Tildy was surprised to notice that Aunt Rachel and Annabelle and Roseanne had changed from the dresses they had been wearing earlier that afternoon. It hardly seemed possible to Tildy, but the dresses they wore at dinner time were even more elaborate than the ones they had on before. Tildy supposed that her aunt and uncle and cousins must be dressed up to go out to a party later in the evening.

When Uncle Caleb finished his soup, he pulled a bell cord near his place at the table. Still not a word was said aloud. Tildy wondered what was going to happen, but nothing did. Once again, Uncle Caleb yanked on the bell cord, this time with obvious impatience. Still no one spoke and still nothing happened. Tildy watched in fascination as Uncle Caleb reached for the cord a third time.

Before he could ring it, Juno hurried through the doorway with a large tray and began making her way around the table collecting the soup bowls from each person's place.

"The next time I ring, Juno," Uncle Caleb said. "I expect for you to come immediately."

"Yes, sir, Mr. Caleb," Juno answered as she continued making her rounds and placing the soup bowls on the tray. "Sorry, Mr. Caleb. I was busy with Summy."

Uncle Caleb did not raise his voice but the tone of it was more disturbing to Tildy than if he had shouted. "My son's name is Sumter."

"Yes, sir, Mr. Caleb. I was busy with Sumter."

"It is Linny's job to look after Sumter. You are responsible for serving dinner."

"Yes, sir, but Linny's feeling a mite dauncy today."

"I don't want to hear excuses, Juno. That girl is just plain lazy and you know it. Her job is feeding Sumter his evening meal and putting him to bed. That is what I expect her to do. Your job is seeing that our dinner is served properly and on time. That is what I expect you to do."

"Linny's really sick this time," Juno said, not pausing as she added skillfully to the pile of soup dishes stacked up on her tray.

Uncle Caleb's yellowish face had begun to take on color even though his voice stayed low and measured. "Don't you dare argue with me."

"Not meaning to argue, sir," Juno said. "Just letting you know. Linny's so dizzy she can't hold the child careful-like. I don't want her to drop that baby. I was just thinking of Summy . . . I mean, Master Sumter, sir."

Unexpectedly Uncle Caleb's fist banged down on the table and made the silverware and crystal glasses jangle. His voice was no longer controlled. "I'll decide what is best for my own son."

Then Uncle Caleb turned on Cato who had stopped pulling the cord that worked the fan. "And you . . . you keep that fan going if you want to eat anything tonight. The peace of my home has been ruined. My meal has been spoiled. Maybe you had both better go without any food tonight."

Tildy sat watching the entire scene with wide eyes. Uncle Caleb's meal was not the only one that had been spoiled. She had no desire to eat at the table with this man who had the power to make other persons so miserable. She started to push her chair back so that she could leave the table. She did not realize that Juno had moved directly behind her to remove Tildy's soup bowl. Tildy accidentally knocked Juno's outstretched arm aside and the half-filled soup spilled over Tildy's dress and onto the carpet.

"You clumsy fool," Uncle Caleb shouted. Tildy couldn't believe that he would speak to her that way. "Look what you've done. Clean up that mess immediately before it ruins the carpet. The rug cost me a pretty penny."

Tildy jumped up from her chair and began to dab at the carpet with her handkerchief.

"What are you doing?" Uncle Caleb demanded.

"I'm trying to clean up the mess as you told me to do," Tildy answered.

"I didn't mean for you to do it. I was talking to Juno. That's her work, not yours."

"But it was my fault that the soup spilled," Tildy tried to explain.

"It doesn't matter whose fault it was. I won't have you doing what Juno is supposed to do."

Juno's black curly hair was near Tildy's own dark brown braids. Tildy heard the black woman whisper to her, "Don't you worry, missy. I'll get this cleaned up in no time."

"But it was my fault," Tildy insisted, all the while thinking that if Uncle Caleb had not been so unreasonable none of this would have happened in the first place.

"Please, missy," Juno said softly. "Be better if you just let me do it."

"What are you saying?" Uncle Caleb demanded. His voice was shrill and high-pitched by now.

"She didn't say anything to you," Tildy said, still dabbing at the soupy carpet. "She was talking to me."

"This is my home. I will not abide impudence . . . not from anyone. Not from you or from my slaves."

"Slaves?" Tildy's voice was far louder than she had intended it to be. "Juno and Cato and Linny aren't your slaves any longer. Don't you know that President Lincoln signed an Emancipation Proclamation? The slaves are free now."

"Tildy, dear," her mother cautioned. "Please do sit down and be quiet."

"Well, well, well," said Uncle Caleb, staring directly at Tildy with steely eyes. "I didn't know we had an expert in our midst."

"Not much of an expert," Cousin Lucius snorted. "Go ahead and tell her, Pa."

Uncle Caleb's thin lips turned upward into a smirking smile. "That great proclamation wasn't worth the paper it was written on. The only slaves that were freed were those down South . . ., the deep South. And, as far as I know, Old Abe ain't president down there. Maryland's a border state and that Emancipation Proclamation don't apply here to our slaves."

"But Congress has voted and passed an amendment freeing the slaves," Tildy continued, despite feeling the pressure of Mother's warning hand on her arm.

At this, Lucius roared with laughter. "The House of Representatives hasn't passed it yet and the states haven't ratified it. Did you know that your own Indiana Senator Hendricks voted against it? Oh, you Northerners! You talk a lot about slavery, but when it comes right down to it that's not what this war is all about. All the North wants is to keep its foot on the neck of the South. Well, you'll find out that we have our rights . . . ."

"Rights!" Tildy was standing now, facing Lucius, her hands on her hips. "My papa fought to make sure everybody would be free. That's what this country stands for. Freedom. Freedom for everybody no matter what color their skin."

"Enough," Caleb Larrabie said. He, too, was standing now. "I will not have this kind of display at my dining table. Gentle folks do not behave in this manner. Persons of good breeding do not discuss politics when they are dining. And, womenfolk do not discuss politics . . . ever! What do they know of such things?"

"Well, I know," Tildy said. "My papa subscribed to the Indianapolis newspaper and I read it, too. And, once my papa took me to hear Mr. Lincoln speak."

With that, Tildy ran from the dining room, through the broad hallway, and outside the house. How could Uncle Caleb talk to her like that? Papa had never treated her as a child. He had talked to her about politics. He wanted her to understand the world around her. And he had let her talk to him. Tildy ran until she stumbled and fell to the ground, her tears obscuring her vision. She hated it here. She hated Uncle Caleb and she hated her skinny, sick-looking cousin Lucius. She hated the way the Larrabies treated Juno and Cato and Linny.

Tildy lay on the ground sobbing. All the hurt of the last few months seemed to spill out. She wished her family had never come here. They would have been much better off staying back in Indiana. Somehow they could have thought of something to do . . . someplace to live . . . someway to earn enough money to keep body and soul together as Mother used to say.

It was almost dark when Tildy returned to the Larrabie house. Juno was lighting the lamps in the sitting room at the back of the long, center entryway hall. Tildy could hear Aunt Rachel's soft voice, but could not make out any of her words. Occasionally, she could hear Mother's voice, too. She didn't know if Uncle Caleb or any of the others were in the sitting room or not. Right now, she didn't want to see or talk to anyone.

Tildy tiptoed up the stairway to the second landing and then up the steep steps to their attic room. She wanted to get into bed and go to sleep and try to forget all about this horrid day as quickly as possible. How could so many awful things have happened in so short a time? It seemed as though she had lived a million years in just a few days.

Tildy poured some water from the large, white pitcher into the basin. She splashed her face, thinking how good the cool water felt against her hot cheeks and swollen eyes. Then she slipped into her cotton gown and got into bed.

Tildy had been in between the cool, soothing sheets only a few moments when she heard the door to the attic room open. She kept her eyes closed as Mother and Elizabeth and Louisa entered. Tildy turned her face to the wall. She could hear Mother whispering to the younger girls as she got them ready for bed. Then, Tildy sensed that Mother had come over to where she was lying and stood by her cot.

"Tildy," Mother said quietly. "I've made our apologies to Uncle Caleb and Aunt Rachel for what happened at dinner time. They were gracious enough to understand that you were very tired from our long journey and probably overwrought."

Tildy pressed her lips together to keep from saying anything she might regret. It made her angry to think of Mother having to make excuses for her, especially when Tildy didn't feel at all ashamed of what she had said. Was it right to have to feel ashamed when you spoke the truth?

"Tomorrow will be a fresh new day. We'll all feel better after a good night's sleep. We can start over as though nothing unpleasant has happened," Mother continued.

Tildy felt a renegade tear squeeze out from between her tightly closed eyelids. Still she could not bring herself to speak.

She felt Mother's hand reach out and touch her gently on the shoulder. "I know it is hard for you, Tildy. It's hard for me as well. But, we are guests in this house. We must respect their ways of doing things whether we understand or like those ways. I know you'll help me by not making things any more difficult than they are already."

Tildy could not stop the sobs that now shook her body. Mother sat down on the edge of the bed and cradled Tildy in her arms.

"Oh, Mother," Tildy said, her tears making her words sound thick and blurry. "What's going to happen to us here?"

5

Tildy was awakened very early the next morning by the sunlight streaming through the small dormer window at the east end of the attic room. From below she could hear the sound of voices outside. She got up and went over to look down into the backyard. There she saw Uncle Caleb and Lucius as they struggled to repair a wheel on their wagon.

Tildy got dressed quickly and went downstairs to breakfast. She was glad that she would not have to face either her cousin or her uncle across the table just yet. Those two seemed to bring out the very worst in her and she was determined to make amends for last night's ugly scene. She wanted to make her mother proud of her, or, at least, not to cause Mother any more embarrassment.

Aunt Rachel and Mother and all the children were already eating as Tildy came into the dining room and quietly found a chair. She ate the cold pone and milk that were served to her by Juno and did not join in the adult's conversation.

"I've spoken to several of the ladies in this neighborhood about you, Becky," Aunt Rachel was telling Mother. "There has not been a really fine seamstress in these parts for a number of years. So, they are all quite anxious to meet you."

"That's very good of you, Rachel," Mother said. "I cannot tell you how much I appreciate all you have done for us."

Aunt Rachel reached out and patted Mother's hand. "On the contrary. It is you who have done things for me. Your being here is like a tonic for me. I do think I am feeling better already."

Mother smiled and it seemed to Tildy this was the first time she had seen her mother look happy in a very long time.

"Actually, I have not really done anything for you," Aunt Rachel continued. "All that was necessary was to show the ladies that lovely lawn dress that you made for me way back . . . " Aunt Rachel paused thoughtfully. "Goodness me, how many years has it been?"

Mother shook her head. "I don't know. More than I care to think about."

"At any rate, when the ladies saw the size of those tiny stitches and how well the seams have held all this time, they each wanted to be first in line for your services."

"When can I get started?"

"Today, if you think you are up to it," Aunt Rachel said. "I hope that won't be rushing you too much. Perhaps you should rest a few days more after your long journey."

"Not at all," Mother said. "I think the sooner I can get to work, the better it will be for all concerned."

"Very well. I have some things I want to show you right after we finish eating. Then, we can go this very morning to meet my neighbor across the way. I think you will like Mrs. Surratt. She is a fine, cultured woman."

"Mary Surratt is a self-righteous hypocrite. That's what she is," said Uncle Caleb coming into the dining room followed by Lucius. "That woman thinks she is better than the rest of the folks hereabouts. She's too proud to whitewash."

Tildy wondered what that meant.

"Mrs. Surratt has always been kind and gracious to me," Aunt Rachel defended her neighbor.

"Well, I've talked to her when she's been anything but gracious," Uncle Caleb said.

"I will admit that she can be firm when it comes to business matters," Aunt Rachel said.

"Downright pushy," Uncle Caleb said. "It isn't womanly."

"Perhaps she has had to be unusually strong to run the family business after her husband died. She hasn't had it easy, you know."

Uncle Caleb didn't reply and Tildy thought the conversation was over as Uncle Caleb turned his attention to his meal. He crumbled the cold pone into a bowl and then poured thick yellow cream and dark syrup over it.

"I've heard she has fed Union troops passing through and she didn't even make a charge for it," Lucius said.

"Mary Surratt is a good Christian woman," Aunt Rachel said. "I expect she'd offer hospitality to anyone who came to her door hungry. Just look at the way she took care of that poor Kallenback family when they needed help."

Uncle Caleb's mouth was full of food and he just shook his head steadily from side to side until he had swallowed enough to be able to speak.

Lucius seemed glad to be able to keep the subject alive. "It does seem strange that with her oldest son Isaac in the Confederate army that she'd be giving free handouts to Union soldiers."

"That's right," Uncle Caleb said, gulping down his food. "I tell you there's something that bothers me about that Mrs. Surratt."

Aunt Rachel seemed to be about to reply, but instead she clamped her lips shut tightly and patted them daintily with the corner of her napkin as though to bring an end to the conversation.

Uncle Caleb wasn't finished though. "Now you just take a look at that brother of hers over at Burches Venture Plantation." Uncle Caleb gestured with his spoon as he talked. "That Zadoc Jenkins is the most outspoken Union man in this county."

Aunt Rachel's face flushed and it seemed she could keep quiet no longer. "Surely you don't blame Mrs. Surratt for the opinions of her brother?"

"Well, blood's a lot thicker 'n water," Uncle Caleb said with a tone that indicated he was now ready to put an end to the discussion.

Aunt Rachel evidently had enough too, for she quickly changed the subject. She turned to Mother and said, "Becky dear, if you've finished with your breakfast, perhaps we could look at those things of mine I told you about. The girls will both be needing some new things for the autumn season. I need your advice." She turned to Uncle Caleb and asked, "Will you please excuse us?"

Uncle Caleb nodded and continued eating.

The two women rose from the table followed by the four younger girls. A tug on the bell cord brought Juno from the other room. She took the little boys with her to the back part of the house.

Although Tildy was very hungry this morning and had not yet finished eating her breakfast, she got up and followed her mother and aunt from the room. She certainly didn't want to be left alone with Uncle Caleb and Lucius for company.

Aunt Rachel led the way through the hall to a downstairs room that she was occupying now that she could no longer climb stairs. She opened a large wardrobe and began to select dresses, which she laid across the bed.

"Now these should fit Elizabeth perfectly," Aunt Rachel said. "And I'm sure it won't take much to alter these for Louisa." Aunt Rachel held a few of the ruffly, be-ribboned creations up in front of the girls. Little Louisa was too young to care much about fancy clothing, but Elizabeth was wide-eyed at the sight of such dresses.

Aunt Rachel turned back to the wardrobe and brought out several dresses of her own. "I'm sure these will do perfectly for you, Becky. We always were about the same size. They were made of excellent fabric and still have lots of wear in them."

Soon Mother's arms were full of hand-me-down clothing.

"Now then, that takes care of you and the two younger girls," Aunt Rachel said. "But since Tildy is older than either Roseanne or Annabelle, I just don't know what to offer as suitable clothing for her. Perhaps you can find something of mine in that bunch of dresses that wouldn't be too difficult for you to cut down for her."

It had taken Tildy a little while to realize just what Aunt Rachel was really doing. Her words seemed innocent enough, but it was what lay behind those words that now came through to Tildy. It must have been when Aunt Rachel talked about finding something *suitable* for Tildy to wear that she knew what was beneath all of this.

Tildy's cheeks burned with humiliation when she thought back to the scene around the Larrabie dinner table last evening. Aunt Rachel and Annabelle and Roseanne had all been dressed so fancily that Tildy was certain they were planning to go to a party. Now, she realized that this was the way the Larrabies dressed for dinner every night.

What Aunt Rachel must really be saying, but not in so many words, was that the Grahams, in homespun and calico, were not suitably attired for the Larrabie table. It evidently didn't matter that they were neat and clean. What was important in this house was that dresses be fancy. The Grahams were too plain. They had no ribbons and lace. They looked like poor relations. Then, Tildy realized with a rush of hot anger that that is exactly what they were.

Tildy felt outraged. Her family was decent and hardworking. They had never taken handouts. Not even from kinfolks.

Tildy couldn't believe it when she heard her mother say, "These are all just lovely, Rachel. Thank you so much."

"I hope you'll be able to wear some of these things at dinner tonight."

"Yes, of course we will," Mother agreed.

Angrily Tildy followed her mother up to their attic room with the new finery.

As soon as the door was closed behind them, Tildy said, "Papa wouldn't have let you take all those dresses Aunt Rachel gave you. You know how he felt about charity."

She was startled when Mother turned to her and said matter of-factly, "Tildy, your papa's not here now. Things have changed. We have to get along the best we can."

Tildy was so stunned by this that she couldn't say anything for a moment. Mother busied herself putting the finery away in their wardrobe. Then, she began to examine one of the dresses that Aunt Rachel suggested could be cut down to fit Tildy.

"You needn't bother to make that dress over for me to wear," Tildy said. "If I'm not good enough to eat at the Larrabie table wearing my own clothing, then having a fancy dress on isn't going to change a thing."

"You're right about that, Tildy," Mother said. "What we wear certainly doesn't make us into different persons, but I am going to alter this dress. And, you are going to wear it."

"I love you, Mother," Tildy said. "but if I can't eat at Uncle Caleb's fine table because I'm wearing homespun, then I'll eat in the kitchen with the rest of his slaves!"

"Matilda Ann Graham, I love you, too," Mother said firmly. "And Aunt Rachel loves us and that is why she gave us these dresses. We will wear them because we love her and do not wish to disrupt the peace of her home."

Tildy could not believe the tone of Mother's voice.

"What do you mean?" Tildy wanted to know.

"I mean that my own dear sister would never think of doing anything to hurt me. If it were up to her, we could come to the table dressed any way we pleased. This is not her decision."

"You mean Uncle Caleb told her to give us those clothes?"

"Not in so many words," Mother said. "But, Aunt Rachel is trying to spare us any more unpleasantness that she can."

Tildy thought about that for a few moments. Try as she would she could not make any real sense of it. She stood quietly glaring at the dress that was to be altered to fit her.

When Tildy didn't speak, Mother said, "I will not cause my sister any unhappiness by doing something that will give her husband a chance to criticize. That would hurt her far more than it will hurt us to wear these clothes. We know in our hearts what is important. I suspect that given a choice, your Aunt Rachel would dress just as we do, but she has to cater to her husband's wishes."

"Then she is as much his slave as Juno or Cato or Linny," Tildy burst out angrily.

"Shhhh." Mother put her fingertips to her lips. "You may not understand just now what it is I am trying to tell you, but do not let your anger make you act in haste. Take time to think things over carefully."

"No matter how long I think about it, I shall never understand how Aunt Rachel could have married a man like Caleb Larrabie. He's so selfish and mean."

"He wasn't always like that," Mother said, and Tildy was certain that she detected a note of sadness in her voice. "He was actually a rather charming young man. We thought he was very good-looking. In fact, all the young ladies we knew were quite taken with him. How they envied Rachel when she was the one he asked to marry him."

"Uncle Caleb?" Tildy asked in amazement. "Well, he surely fooled everybody, didn't he?"

"No, I don't think he fooled us. He was very different back then. He was so full of plans about the future and the kind of life he wanted to provide for Rachel."

"Then why is he like this?"

"Sometimes unforeseen things happen that can embitter a person and make them change."

"What kind of things could change a truly nice person into the man Uncle Caleb is now?"

"In his case, things like losing a dream. Things like working hard for years only to lose everything."

"Kind of like what happened to us when we lost our farm back in Indiana?" Tildy asked and then, seeing the look of pain flutter across Mother's face, she wished immediately that she had not brought that into the conversation.

"I don't know that the two situations can be compared," Mother said. "We lost the farm because we couldn't work it by ourselves without a man."

"What happened to Uncle Caleb?" Tildy was eager to change the subject.

"It's a very long story," Mother said. "But the first thing that happened was shortly after Caleb and another man went into business together. He worked very hard and the future looked bright. He and Rachel got married. The business was making a lot of money, so they bought a fine house. Then, one day his partner ran away, taking all the money. Uncle Caleb was left to pay off their debts. He lost his store, the fine house, and everything."

"That's terrible," Tildy cried.

"You're right," Mother agreed. "But, he was determined to make it up to Rachel. They moved to Kentucky and bought a farm. Again he worked very hard and things looked good. Two years later, he lost everything again because of a faulty land title. It seems that the man he bought the place from didn't own it free and clear. Once again all his hard work went for nothing and he lost everything through no fault of his own. He felt as though he had failed his wife and children."

For a moment, Tildy felt sorry for Uncle Caleb. She knew how terrible it was to lose something you had worked hard for.

Mother continued her story. "For the next few years Caleb had to hire out and work for other people. Your Aunt Rachel took in washing and did other people's ironing. They scrimped and saved and went without things in order to get enough money to start over again. They were finally able to move to Maryland and buy this place a few years ago. It's really more than he and Lucius can handle, even with the help of Cato and Juno and Linny. They still have to scratch to make ends meet. Aunt Rachel worries because they are always just one step ahead of the bill collector."

Tildy sighed with exasperation. "Then why does Uncle Caleb insist on everyone wearing all those fancy clothes? And why do they have such grand furnishings? I've never seen anything as fancy as their parlor and dining room. Why does he waste money on such things when they don't really need them and can't afford them?"

"Caleb Larrabie is a proud man," Mother said. "He vowed he would make up all the sacrifices to his wife and children."

"Why doesn't Aunt Rachel just put her foot down and tell him they don't need so many things to be happy?"

Mother sat silently for a moment before she said, "Aunt Rachel loves her husband. She understands how hurt he has been. If you've looked about you will notice that it's only the front two rooms of this house that are so grandly furnished."

Tildy was surprised to realize that what Mother had just said was true. Aunt Rachel's bedroom and the rooms where the Larrabie children slept were all very plain. Tildy had thought that Uncle Caleb had put her and her mother and sisters in that simple little attic room because he didn't want them here.

"So, Uncle Caleb only fixes up the rooms that visitors might see and dresses his family in fine clothing to impress other people."

"I suppose that might be one way to look at it," Mother said.

"Do you remember what Uncle Caleb said about their neighbor Mrs. Surratt?" Tildy asked.

"He said several things if I recall correctly."

77

"I mean the part about her being a hypocrite," Tildy said. "And he said she thought she was better than other people. And what did he mean when he said she was too proud to whitewash?"

Mother smiled that sad little smile again and nodded. "Yes, I remember that. Poor Caleb. He does tend to overdo things. Aunt Rachel told me privately that he had to sell one of his horses in order to buy white paint for this house. You see, he wouldn't stoop to whitewash either because that's what poor folks have to do."

"Sounds to me like he's the hypocrite," Tildy said. "He . . . ."

Mother reached out and put her hand on Tildy's arm. "Be careful, Tildy. Let's not be too quick with our criticism of him. I find it's hard enough to live my own life well without trying to direct others."

"But Uncle Caleb directs others," Tildy cried out. "He thinks everybody ought to do exactly what he says. Wouldn't you think that a person who had been treated so unfairly himself would try to be nice to other people? Instead he is so awful to Juno and Cato and Linny. Can't he understand how they feel? Doesn't he care?"

"Oh, my dear Tildy. Part of what I love so much about you is your strong sense of what is right and wrong. In that, you are so much like your papa was." Mother paused and sighed. "But, I am afraid that is what will make life very hard for you sometimes."

Tildy couldn't help but ask, "Was life hard for Papa?"

"Oh, yes," Mother said. "There were times when life was very hard indeed. You see, he always insisted on

78

doing exactly what he thought was right, no matter what anybody else thought."

Tildy was almost afraid to ask the next question, but even more afraid not to. "You did love Papa, didn't you?"

Mother leaned back and laughed and then her eyes got that far-away look in them. "Yes, Tildy. I loved your papa more than anything else in this world, but . . .," she paused, "that didn't always make things easier."

6

Mother left their attic bedroom to go back down-stairs. Their long talk had given Tildy much to think about. She still wasn't certain she understood it all. She went over to look out of the attic window. Below she could see that Uncle Caleb and Lucius and Cato had returned to the task of trying to repair the wagon wheel. There, the three of them labored side by side. Tildy had no doubt that Uncle Caleb worked as hard or even harder than either of the two boys. In that way he was a lot like Papa. But whereas at the end of the day Papa had liked nothing better than to talk and laugh and enjoy being with his family, Uncle Caleb dressed up in his fine clothes and pretended he was master of a great planta-tion. Tildy was sure she knew what Papa would think of that kind of pretension.

Suddenly, Tildy remembered that Mother and Aunt Rachel had planned to make a call on Mrs. Surratt today. Tildy certainly didn't want to miss out on that opportu-nity, especially after what she had heard about the woman over breakfast this morning. Tildy wanted to see for herself and make up her own mind.

Tildy clattered down the narrow steps to the second floor landing. There she found Linny leading the six younger Larrabies plus Elizabeth and Louisa as they came upstairs.

"Have they gone yet?" Tildy asked as she tried to squeeze past the small flock. "Aunt Rachel and Mother, I mean. Have they gone to Mrs. Surratt's?"

"Yes, ma'am," Linny said, grabbing at little Summy to keep him from falling. "Left a while back."

"We're going to play school," Elizabeth called to Tildy. "Come and play with us."

But Tildy had already reached the bottom of the steps and was into the entryway hall. She started toward the front door but almost bumped into Juno who was coming out of the parlor.

Before Tildy had a chance to ask, Juno said, "Back door's the quickest way to Surratt's. They went across the field."

Tildy turned around and dashed through the hall to the back. Behind her she could hear Juno muttering something about "living with a whirlwind."

Tildy burst out into the bright sunshine at the rear of the house. She looked about but couldn't see any sign of Mother or Aunt Rachel. Uncle Caleb, Lucius, and Cato all glanced up at her.

"How do I get to Mrs. Surratt's house?" Tildy asked.

Uncle Caleb turned back to his work without answering, but Lucius said, "That way, but you'll never catch up with them now."

"Oh yes I will," Tildy said and grabbed hold of her full skirts so that she would not trip over them and set off across the fallow field like a coon being chased by hound dogs.

Tildy managed to reach the Surratt place just as Mother and Aunt Rachel were getting ready to walk up the few steps to the porch.

"Tildy!" Mother said, as she turned and saw her.

"Mercy me," Aunt Rachel gasped. "You didn't run all that distance, did you?"

Tildy could only nod as she was so out of breath.

"And no hat on either." Aunt Rachel held her little parasol over Tildy to shade her. "Do sit down on that stump and rest before you collapse. Why, it exhausts me just to look at you."

"Tildy, you are a sight." Mother took her handkerchief from her pocket and patted the dampness from Tildy's hot face."

"I feel fine," Tildy insisted, wishing all this fussing over her would stop. Actually, Tildy felt wonderful. It was so good to stretch her legs at last. That was what legs were for, not to sit around as she had been doing the past week. "I'm only a bit winded from having been lazy so long."

"Your hair is flying all over." Mother tucked the loose ends behind Tildy's ears and tried to smooth the front with her hands.

As Mother and Aunt Rachel hovered about trying to make her more presentable, Tildy had an opportunity to take a good look at the Surratt house. Uncle Caleb had been right about one thing. It was quite weather-beaten and could even use a coat of whitewash. If it had been her place, Tildy decided, she wouldn't let pride keep her from improving it in whatever way she could afford.

"Are we ready to go inside now?" Aunt Rachel wanted to know.

"Yes," Mother said. "I think her color is back to normal now." Mother continued to fan Tildy with her hankie. "Her face isn't quite so red."

As they climbed the steps onto the porch, Tildy could hear the sound of a piano being played somewhere in the house. As Aunt Rachel knocked, the music stopped abruptly. The door was opened and they were greeted by a tall, well-proportioned young woman.

"Good morning, Mrs. Larrabie. Do come in. My mother has been expecting you."

"Thank you, Anna," Aunt Rachel said. "I would like for you to meet my sister, Rebecca Graham, and her daughter Matilda. Becky, this is Anna, Mrs. Surratt's daughter."

Anna led the way to the family parlor at the right of the entry. Tildy noticed that the room to the left was outfitted as a country store. All sorts of goods were for sale. Saddles, harnesses, and hams were suspended from ceiling hooks. There were containers of peppermint candy and flour as well as salt, fish, and tobacco in casks. Through another door beyond the store Tildy caught sight of a post office and a tavern area.

"Tildy, don't gawk around like that," Mother whispered as Mrs. Surratt came toward them.

Tildy thought that Mrs. Surratt seemed to be a pleasant enough woman. She had dark hair, which she parted in the center and wore draped over her ears and caught up at the back in a bun. She had an oval face and her eyes, although she seemed to squint as she looked at Tildy, were kind eyes. Like her daughter Anna, Mrs. Surratt was tall. She held herself very straight as she walked. Did that mean she was the proud woman that Uncle Caleb accused her of being?

Mrs. Surratt reached out and grasped both of Aunt Rachel's hands in her own and said, "I am so glad to see you, Rachel. How are you feeling? I do hope it wasn't too much for you to walk across the field? Perhaps I should have come to your home, but . . . well, you know how awkward it is."

Tildy wondered if Mrs. Surratt had been reluctant to come to the Larrabie's because of Uncle Caleb.

Aunt Rachel laughed just a bit and said, "I am much better now that my dear sister and her little family are here. And, I think it is good for me to get out of the house once in a while. Yours is the only place I can come to where no one will see me. I do find it so difficult to have to stay shut up at home during confinement."

"Yes, I recall how lonely I used to be at that time, too." Mrs. Surratt motioned in the direction of a comfortable chair. "Do sit down now and rest."

After another round of introductions, Mrs. Surratt turned to Mother and said, "Your sister has given us glowing reports of what a fine seamstress you are. I am so pleased that you have moved here. Both Anna and I have been needing some new things made. Also, I have several garments that urgently require mending. I'm afraid my eyesight is becoming so much worse everyday I cannot even see to thread a needle."

As the conversation turned into a lengthy discussion of the clothing that Mrs. Surratt wanted Mother to make, Tildy listened to their soft voices. She thought that she had never heard anyone speak as did Mrs. Surratt and Anna. Even though Tildy occasionally had a difficult time making out a word or two because of the slightly different inflection than she was accustomed to, Tildy couldn't help but thinking she liked the sound of their talk. They were so gracious and polite. It hardly fit Uncle Caleb's uncomplimentary description. In fact, Tildy was quite entranced by the woman and her daughter.

"In addition to the dresses, I shall probably want a new cloak," Mrs. Surratt was saying. "Anna and I will be moving into the city before long."

"Moving?" Aunt Rachel asked in surprise. "Why, I had no idea that you planned such a thing."

"Yes," Mrs. Surratt said. "I think it would be better for Johnny." Mrs. Surratt turned to Mother to explain. "Johnny is my youngest son, John Junior. I think things will be more hopeful for him in Washington City."

"It just won't seem the same without you in the neighborhood," Aunt Rachel said.

"Washington isn't all that far away now, is it? And, I shall be back to visit and take care of my business here from time to time."

"Then you plan to keep the store and post office here as before?"

"Oh yes," Mrs. Surratt assured here. "I will find someone to run the business for me. It is nothing but a bare living and so won't do for Johnny, but I am not ready to sell it just yet."

"Well, I'm glad to hear that you'll not be breaking your ties to our community," Aunt Rachel said. "Have you found a place to live in Washington?"

"There's a large house on 'H' Street. I think it will serve quite well as a boardinghouse. That should provide an extra bit of money for me. I understand that there is a shortage of suitable rooms for visitors to the capital city."

"Of course, we shall expect you to visit us whenever you come back here," Aunt Rachel said.

"You can be assured that I will," Mrs. Surratt promised.

The conversation then turned briefly back to the clothing that the Surratts would need. Mother took some measurements and quickly estimated the amount of fabric she would require to make up the order.

After that business had been attended to, Mrs. Surratt turned to her daughter. "Anna, dear, would you be good enough to bring tea for us into the parlor now?"

Anna left the room briefly and returned with a large tray generously filled with a variety of good things to eat.

"I'll have Anna fill a little basket of goodies for you to take back to your house for the little ones who didn't come with you," Mrs. Surratt said.

Then, Mrs. Surratt turned her attention to Tildy. "Has it been decided where you will go to school, my dear?"

Tildy was surprised to have Mrs. Surratt draw her into the conversation. According to Uncle Caleb, a girl her age had nothing to say that would be of interest to anyone.

"I suppose I'll go to school where the other boys and girls go," Tildy said, realizing for the first time that they hadn't given any thought to it.

"There is a very fine seminary for young ladies not many miles from here," Mrs. Surratt said. "Anna went there and received an excellent education."

Anna smiled. "Oh yes, I'm sure you would like it. They offer so many interesting courses of study."

"Is that where you learned to play the piano?" Tildy asked.

"How did you know that I play the piano?" Anna asked.

"We heard the music when we arrived," Tildy said. "It was so beautiful. I think it would be wonderful to be able to play the piano as you do."

"Perhaps you would like for Anna to play something for you now?" Mrs. Surratt asked.

"We'd like that very much, wouldn't we?" Tildy asked Mother and Aunt Rachel.

"Do play something," Mother encouraged.

Anna sat at the piano and began to play a lovely tune that she said was called "Kathleen Mavourneen." She followed this with another, called "Lorena."

Tildy marveled that Anna played without looking at any musical score. In fact, as the young woman began the third melody, Tildy noticed that Anna's eyes were focused firmly on a picture that was hanging over the piano.

"Do play something livelier," Mrs. Surratt suggested.

Tildy had to admit that she was glad when Anna began the notes to "Sweet Evalina." The other songs had made her feel quite sad.

When at last Tildy and her mother and aunt left the Surratt place, she walked on ahead of Mother and Aunt Rachel. She wanted to be by herself. Even the brisk notes of the last tune could not erase the melancholy feeling left by the first few songs Anna had played. Tildy was sure that Anna had played the sad songs with much greater emotion than she had the last number. Tildy had a feeling that somehow the plaintive music and the picture were bound up together.

When they arrived back at the Larrabie's, Aunt Rachel went to her room to rest for a while. Mother suggested that Tildy go upstairs and freshen up after all her exertions. Tildy climbed the stairs up to the second floor landing. Before she could open the door leading to the attic steps, it flew open and Lucius stepped out. He seemed as startled to see her standing there as she had been to find him coming from the flight of stairs that led to the Graham's third floor room.

He looked at her with a strange expression about his lips. "I took your water pitcher and basin up to your room," he said. "Juno had emptied it and I told her I would save her a trip back upstairs."

"Thank you," Tildy said, surprised by her cousin's sudden friendliness.

"How do you like our neighbors?" Lucius asked.

"I thought they were very nice," Tildy said. "They couldn't have been more hospitable." She was tempted to add that they did not seem at all to be what Uncle Caleb had said they were. "They were friendly and accepted us just as though we had been friends for years."

That odd expression played about the corners of Lucius' mouth again. Tildy tried to figure it out but was hard-pressed to come up with a word for it.

"I wonder how well you would like them if you knew what I know?" Lucius asked.

"Just what do you know?" Tildy asked, beginning to feel irritated with him.

Lucius didn't answer but stood staring at Tildy for a moment. He then turned and started down the stairway to the entryway on the main floor.

Tildy was about to go up to her room when Lucius turned back and said to her, "By the way, did Anna show you her favorite picture? The one over the piano?"

Even though it was very warm, Tildy shivered as she walked away from her cousin and started up the stairway to the third floor room.

It wasn't until she was up in her room that Tildy began to think about what Lucius had said when she caught him coming down the attic stairway. He had told her that he had brought their water pitcher and basin upstairs to save Juno a trip. She had been so astonished to see him that she had accepted his explanation at first. The more she thought about it, the more she questioned his words. She remembered that when she had started over to the Surratt place, Lucius had been helping his father with the wagon. Strange that Uncle Caleb would have allowed him to stop that and come into the house to help Juno with her work. And, she had not noticed that Uncle Caleb or Lucius ever did anything to save Juno any extra steps.

Tildy looked about the attic room wondering what Lucius had really been up to. It was then that she knew exactly how to describe the look she had seen on Lucius' face a little while ago. It was sly and furtive. She knew that she did not trust her cousin. Not one bit.

7

"Tildy, please quit fidgeting that way," Mother said. "You will scar Aunt Rachel's furniture swinging your feet back and forth against it that way."

Tildy had not even been aware that she had been bumping the heels of her shoes on the leg of the dining room chair.

Tildy sighed and tried to sit still as she helped Mother, who had spread out her sewing on the long table. But, try as she would Tildy could not help being restless. Life here in Maryland at the Larrabie's was totally different than it had been back on their farm in Indiana. There, Tildy had been outside working in the fresh air as much as possible. Here, in Surrattsville, she felt housebound—almost like a prisoner.

Tildy would much rather have been doing almost anything else, anywhere else as Mother painstakingly cut out the fine, white, bleached muslin for Mrs. Surratt's new petticoats. She had tried standing on the back porch where Uncle Caleb might suggest some yard work for her to do, but he had made it clear that he didn't need or want her help and he wished that she would get out from underfoot. So, she had gone back inside the house to the dining room where Mother was working. Tildy felt that it was her duty to help Mother sew, even though it had long ago been acknowledged that stitchery was not one of Tildy's special talents.

It annoyed Tildy more than a little bit that Elizabeth seemed quite content to sit quietly on a chair next to her two cousins embroidering as they were doing.

Not only did Elizabeth seem to enjoy following the lead of Annabelle and Roseanne, she also seemed to be happy to be dressed up the way they were. She delighted in wearing the flounces, ribbons, and laces that had once been theirs.

Even worse, Tildy was distressed when Elizabeth had whined and pouted evening before last when it was time for her to go to bed. Elizabeth had insisted that Mother wrap her hair in rag curlers so that she could have ringlets just like those of Annabelle and Roseanne.

"Mother is tired," Tildy had tried to explain to her younger sister. "She has been sewing all day long. You mustn't ask her to fix your hair."

"Then I shall get Linny to do it," Elizabeth insisted. "She does Annabelle's and Roseanne's hair every night. And, she combs it out every morning, too."

"That's all the more reason for you not to ask Linny," Tildy said. "Linny has more than enough children to look after each day without being expected to add you to her responsibilities."

Elizabeth had cried and cried and cried until Mother agreed to wrap the curlers for her. In the end, however, it was Tildy herself who spent the better part of an hour painstakingly twisting the white rags tightly around sections of Elizabeth's hair and tying it in floppy white bows.

The next morning, Elizabeth had awakened cross and grumpy because the knotted rags had been hard to sleep on. Tildy was equally cross because Elizabeth's tossing and turning had kept her awake all night.

"You're hurting me," Elizabeth wailed as Tildy brushed out the frizzy mass of hair and tried to fashion it into ringlets.

Secretly, Tildy was pleased for she hoped that Elizabeth would see the stupidity of suffering so much just to have curls. Surely that would be the end of it, but the next night Elizabeth again insisted on the same rag curlers.

"I want rag curls, too," Louisa had chimed in.

Even Mother had finally run out of patience with her younger daughters. "If you girls want curls, you will just have to learn to wrap them on your own . . . and brush them out yourself."

Louisa had gone off to try to curl her rag doll's hair, but Elizabeth had stormed and cried until Tildy had said angrily, "Mother, she has never acted this way before. I think Annabelle and Roseanne are a bad influence on her."

Mother didn't reply, but the way she pressed her lips tightly together told Tildy that Mother didn't like this turn of events either. Mother took Elizabeth firmly by the arm and led her to bed.

Tildy said, "If that is what Uncle Caleb means by raising his daughters to be perfect little ladies, then I think we ought to become hooligans."

"Tildy!" Mother said sharply, "Enough of that. Haven't I enough worries? You've gone to the other extreme."

Tildy immediately felt sorry and promised to try and be more helpful in the future.

So it had gone, day after day, with Tildy becoming more and more frustrated. She tried to make herself sit quietly for hours, beside her mother, sewing. Inwardly she fumed, brooding and thinking how unfair it was that they should have lost the farm and be forced to live like this. The more Tildy brooded, the more careless her stitches became.

"Ouch!" she howled as she punctured her finger with the needle and a circle of bright red blood spurted from her finger onto the fine, white muslin.

"Oh, Tildy dear," Mother exclaimed, the exasperation evident in her voice. "Not again!"

Tildy nodded. "I'm afraid so."

"Give me the cloth quickly," Mother said. "I've got to get it washed out before it stains. I thought I could count on you to do this basting."

"Tildy doesn't like to sew as much as I do," Elizabeth said to Annabelle and Roseanne, both of whom put down their embroidery and stared at Tildy as though she were some sort of circus freak.

"You girls tend to your own needlework," Aunt Rachel said softly but firmly.

Tildy waited in silence for Mother to return. The sound of the ticking of the tall clock in the entryway emphasized each long minute.

"I think it is going to be all right. I can't see a mark on the cloth."

"Mother, I'm sorry," Tildy tried to apologize.

Mother sat down in her chair and looked at Tildy across the table. "I think perhaps it would be better for all concerned if you found something else to do for a while."

"Yes, Mother," Tildy said, feeling half ashamed and half relieved to be released from the task of sewing. She got up and went through the entry hall and opened the front door to go outside.

"There are hats on the hall tree," Elizabeth called to her. "Be sure to cover up. The sun is hot."

Tildy started to reply to her meddlesome sister but then decided it would be best simply to ignore Elizabeth's warning. It was enough for Tildy to set her jaw firmly and leave the house without putting on a hat. What did she care if she got a few more freckles on her nose? She certainly had no desire to become a southern belle with fish-belly white skin. Nothing seemed less appealing to her than sitting around in a parlor all day, looking sickly. It made her angry that Elizabeth had so quickly taken up the silly, simpering ways of her Maryland cousins.

Now that Tildy had escaped the sewing session, she stood on the front porch of the Larrabie house not quite knowing what to do. She felt so completely out of place here. She had never been good at doing those things that people called "women's work." What she was good at was helping Papa.

She felt the quick rush of tears stinging her eyelids and she jumped down off the front porch and walked around to the back of the house.

Juno was out in back, singing as she worked the churn.

"What're you doing, child?" the black woman called to her.

Ordinarily, she would have enjoyed talking with Juno, maybe even taking her turn at the churn. Right now, though, Tildy did not want to see or talk to anybody. Her unhappiness had created such a lump in her throat that she couldn't even answer the friendly Juno.

Tildy started to run aimlessly. Her long skirts whipping about her legs. She ran, not knowing where she was going. She ran out across the back lot and past the outbuildings. She just kept running and didn't stop until she was in a wooded area beyond the field. It was nice here in the shade of the trees. She wiped her sleeve across her forehead and inhaled a deep breath of fresh air. It felt good, even if it was hot. She leaned back and shook her head wishing her hair were not bound up. She was just about to take out the pins and undo the braid, which had been coiled in buns over her ears, when she heard a sound. She listened and realized there were voices in the brushy area just beyond. She walked slowly toward the sound, pausing behind a tree trunk so that she wouldn't be seen.

She recognized one of the voices as belonging to Uncle Caleb. The other was that of Cato. Tildy crept forward to a place where she could see them. They had been cutting wood. A large pile of logs littered a small clearing in the trees.

"I'm going on back to the barn," Uncle Caleb was saying to Cato. "You load this wood on the wagon and drive it back to the house."

Cato nodded.

"Mind you, now. I don't want you sneaking off and taking a nap the minute my back is turned," Uncle Caleb said. "If all this wood isn't stacked up nice and neat back at the house when I come up for dinner, you're going to be one mighty hungry boy tonight. You understand?"

Cato nodded again.

Uncle Caleb started to walk away and then turned back once more, "I mean what I say."

Cato nodded one more time.

Tildy watched until she was certain Uncle Caleb was out of sight. Cato was carrying the cut logs to the wagon as he had been ordered. Tildy walked out into the clearing and picked up a log. She carried it over to the wagon and placed it beside the one Cato had just loaded.

Cato turned and looked at her with startled eyes. "Here, what's that you're doing?"

"I'm helping you load up this wood," Tildy said.

"You're not supposed to be doing that," Cato said.

"Why not?" Tildy asked, turning back to go and get another log.

Cato seemed astounded at her lack of understanding, "'Cause, you're white folks."

"Are you trying to tell me that white folks don't know how to stack wood?" She carried the log to the wagon and dropped it on the stack.

"Besides, you're a girl," Cato said.

"I may be a girl but many a time I helped my papa cut and stack wood on our farm back in Indiana."

"What's Indiana?" Cato wanted to know.

"That's where we lived before we came here."

Cato seemed to have no further curiosity about it. "You better get yourself somewhere else. If Master Caleb come back here and see what you're doing, he's gonna be mad like you never saw mad before."

"He's gone back to the barn," Tildy said. "I waited until I was sure of that."

"Well, you best not get in my way," Cato said. "If I don't get this here wood back to that house and get it stacked by supper, I'm gonna be in bad trouble."

"I know," Tildy said. "That's why I'm helping you. I think you'd be glad to have my help."

"I just don't want no trouble."

"I'm not going to cause any trouble," Tildy said. "All I'm doing is helping you load up this wood."

Cato sighed and shook his head. He went back to work, muttering something she couldn't make out. The two of them worked side by side in the damp heat. Tildy felt her clothing sticking to her uncomfortably. She would have given anything for a drink of water.

"Aren't you thirsty?" she asked Cato.

"Course I am," he said. "There's water up to the house. When I finish here's when I get my drink."

Cato and Tildy continued to carry and load, passing each other as they went back and forth to the wagon.

"How old are you?" Tildy asked.

"Don't know," he said.

"I'll bet you're about my age. Have you ever been to school?"

Cato seemed to think that was funny and laughed. "No reason to," he said.

"Can you read?"

"Course I can't read."

"That's why you ought to go to school," Tildy said.

"Black folks don't need no reading."

"Everybody needs to know how to read," Tildy insisted.

"What am I gonna read?"

"You can read books and newspapers."

"What for?"

"So you'll know what's going on."

"I know what's going on," he said. "What's going on is that I got to get this here wood stacked up at the house or I don't get no supper."

"And what happens when this war is over and you don't have to do what Mr. Caleb tells you to do?" Tildy asked.

"Don't know nothing about that," Cato said.

"Well, you'd know about it if you could read."

Cato didn't answer.

"Have you ever heard about President Lincoln?" Tildy asked.

"You sure are full of questions," Cato said, pausing for a moment to wipe his forehead.

"Well, have you heard of him?" Tildy wasn't going to be put off by his resistance.

"Yep, I heard of him."

"And just what have you heard?" Tildy pressed on with her examination.

"I heard . . . I heard . . . I just heard things."

"I suppose you heard bad things from Uncle Caleb or Lucius," Tildy said. "Well, if you could read, you would find out for yourself what Mr. Lincoln is trying to do."

Cato stopped his work only for a moment to look at her as though he were trying to figure her out, but he didn't say anything, one way or another.

Tildy was undaunted. "Mr. Lincon is a good man. He's trying to help you."

"Why'd he be trying to help me? He don't know me."

"Of course, he doesn't know you, Cato," Tildy said. "But he is trying to help you."

"Don't make no sense," Cato said. "Don't make no sense that if he don't know me he wants to help me."

Tildy couldn't think of a way to explain it to him, so she continued to carry the logs. At least, she thought, working hard made her feel better. It was something she could do.

The sun was sinking lower in the sky when they finished loading all the logs on the wagon. Cato climbed up onto the wagon seat and took the reins. He looked back down at Tildy where she stood in the clearing.

"How you getting back to the house?"

Tildy felt certain that he was nervous about taking her along in the wagon with him.

"I'll walk," she said, wanting to release him from feeling any responsibility for her. "You get going."

"You been working hard. It's still hot out across them fields. You can't walk."

"I can walk," Tildy assured him. "I'm used to hard work and walking. I'm not like Annabelle and Roseanne."

"What if you get sick walking back to the house?" he wanted to know.

"Listen, Cato," Tildy said. "If I ride back to the house with you on the wagon, Uncle Caleb might see us. Then, you'd get into trouble, wouldn't you?"

Cato sat quietly for a moment. Then he nodded.

"You go, I tell you," Tildy said. "I will be all right."

"You say that Mr. Lincoln's really a good man and he wants to help me?"

"That's right," Tildy said.

"You know that Mr. Lincoln face-to-face?"

"My papa took me to hear him make a speech and I've read about him," Tildy said. "Now, you better get going. It's almost supper time."

Cato made a clicking sound with his tongue and the

horse moved slowly ahead pulling the wagonload of wood. Cato turned once and looked back at her. Tildy smiled and waved. Cato waved back at her. He was smiling, too.

Tildy sat down by a tree and waited until Cato and the wagon were out of sight before she left the wooded area. Slowly she walked across the fields and back to the Larrabie house. She paused in the backyard at the pump and splashed her face in the cool water. She smoothed back her hair.

"If my pa finds out what you were doing out in the woods with Cato, there'll be trouble," said a voice behind her.

She whirled to find Lucius standing there, his hands on his hips, his face covered with his usual sly grin.

"Who said I was out in the woods with Cato?"

"I say it. I've got ways of knowing."

"Well, if you're so smart and know so much, you know that all I did was to help him load up some wood."

"Loading wood is Cato's job, not yours. You shouldn't have been helping him."

"You Larrabies! You think you're such proper folks," Tildy lashed out at her cousin. "Well, if you've got such good breeding then you ought to know that a guest in your home is supposed to be allowed to do whatever she chooses to do to amuse herself."

"Well now, you're not exactly a guest here, are you?" Lucius said.

"What is that supposed to mean?"

"It means that you and your mother and your two sisters don't have any place else to go. You're here because we had to take you in."

Tildy was so angry the words fairly burst from her. "My mother is paying for every bite of food we eat. She's working to earn our keep. We're not on charity here."

"You all couldn't afford any other place to live," he insisted.

"Your mother invited us here. What do you think she would do if she knew that you were talking like this to me?" Tildy demanded.

"What do you think my pa would say if he knew what you were talking about to Cato while you were out in the woods?"

"And just what was I saying?"

"You were talking to him about Old Abe and about going to school and learning to read. That kind of thing."

"You were out there spying on me," Tildy was outraged.

Lucius kept grinning. "You think you're helping Cato, but you're just making things hard for him."

"I'm not the one who's making things hard for him," Tildy said. "You're the ones who have made slaves of these people."

"Cato and Juno and Linny are happy here," Lucius said. "We take care of them. They've got a place to live and food to eat. Sure they work hard. So do I and so does my pa."

"But they're not free to come and go as they please."

"Just where would they go?" Lucius asked. "If they were free, they'd probably just stay around here and do the same kind of work they're doing now. They don't know any other kind of life."

"Things are going to be different when this war is

over," Tildy said. "You're in for a big surprise if you don't change your way of thinking."

Lucius laughed. "Maybe you're the one who's in for a big surprise."

Tildy thought Lucius' eyes suddenly took on an unusual glitter.

"You don't really think you Rebels can win the war?" Tildy taunted. "General Grant has Petersburg under siege. The South is almost done for. They haven't got enough men to keep fighting. Why, I've read that in some places there are boys your age who are soldiers."

Tildy was surprised at the sudden change of expression on Lucius' face. He seemed to flinch as though she had struck him.

He was no longer smiling when he said, "There are lots of ways to fight. Not everybody can be a soldier." Then he added ominously, "There are things going on that you could never guess in a million years."

"Like what?" Tildy demanded.

"Like . . . like . . ." Lucius stammered. "Secret things. Things I can't talk about."

Tildy laughed out loud. "You're just full of big talk Lucius Larrabie. If you really knew anything important, you'd tell it right out."

Lucius' thin cheeks were getting redder by the minute. "Just you wait."

"How long am I going to have to wait?" Tildy sensed that she had backed him into a corner.

"One week," Lucius said. "One week from today and you and everybody else will know what the secret is. Then you'll see that the Confederacy isn't done for. You'll see. Everybody will see."

8

The next week came and went. The important date on which Lucius had promised that his great secret would be revealed passed. Everything seemed much the same as it had been before his prediction. In fact, Tildy did not even remember that Lucius had bragged about something momentous happening . . . something so noteworthy that people would change their minds about the South fighting for a lost cause.

Something momentous did happen in the neighborhood, but it had nothing to do with Lucius' boast. It all started with the flurry of excitement about the stray horses.

That was the day that Anna Surratt came hurrying across the field between their place and the Larrabie's. She was waving her hat and calling out, "Mr. Larrabie. Mr. Larrabie. Please come. We need your help."

Tildy had seen Uncle Caleb, Lucius, and Cato emerge from the barn where they had been working.

"Here now, what's all the ruckus?" Uncle Caleb had asked. Anna was so flustered that she could hardly catch her breath long enough to say, "There are wild horses running all through my mother's vegetable patch."

Uncle Caleb grabbed a coil of rope and called to the two boys, "Come on, Lucius and Cato. I may need your help."

The three of them followed Anna back across the field to her house. Tildy had dashed outside when she heard the noise. She trailed along behind Lucius and Cato hoping that Uncle Caleb would not notice her in the commotion.

There was complete confusion at the Surratt's place. Mrs. Surratt's young field hand was running about waving his arms and shouting as he tried to drive the frightened horses from the garden. Mrs. Surratt was calling instructions to him. Several neighborhood boys and their dogs had come over to watch the show. It wasn't long before they, too, decided to join in chasing the terrified animals. All of this noise and activity was causing them to become even more skittish.

"Everyone stand back and be quiet," Uncle Caleb commanded as he created a large loop at the end of his rope. "You boys get hold of your dogs and keep them out of here."

Tildy noticed that all the boys did exactly as Uncle Caleb had told them.

"Ho, now. Whoa, now," Uncle Caleb kept talking to the horses as he moved steadily toward one of them. He held his lasso ready. "Settle down. Steady now. Steady. Steady."

He tossed the loop at the horse's head and missed. Quickly, he reformed the circle of rope and moved in again. All the time he kept talking very quietly to the horse he was attempting to catch. Once more he missed with the rope. The horse reared up on its hind legs, pawing the air frantically. Its eyes were rolled back so that Tildy could see only the whites. She felt certain that the horse would trample Uncle Caleb, but he stepped out of the way. When the horse came back down to the ground, he moved in and deftly passed the rope around its neck.

When the horse felt the rope, it reared again and again. Then the horse dragged Uncle Caleb behind him, but the determined man held fast to the rope. All the time his voice remained controlled and soothing. Tildy was amazed at Uncle Caleb's strength and the way he handled the horse. At last, the skittish animal quieted down.

Uncle Caleb led the horse to the fence rail and securely tied it up.

"I'll need another rope," Uncle Caleb called out and Mrs. Surratt's field hand ran to fetch it.

Uncle Caleb managed to catch the second horse on his first attempt. With those two settled down, the other three horses seemed to calm somewhat. Before long, Uncle Caleb had all five horses where he wanted them.

"Open the barn doors," he directed. "Now, some of you standing around, help me lead them inside."

It wasn't until he was closing the barn doors that Uncle Caleb noticed that Tildy had been one of those who helped bring the horses inside. She had gentled it and patted its nose and spoken softly and it followed her placidly. How good it felt to Tildy to be able to work with a horse again. How much she missed good Old Maud.

When Uncle Caleb did notice that she was helping, he just looked at her but he didn't say a word. She was relieved that he didn't scold her for doing something that he considered, "men's work." He didn't scold her, but he didn't thank her either.

"Mrs. Surratt," Uncle Caleb said when the excitement was all over. "What should we do with these horses? They're not wild, you know. They're strays."

"I suppose we had best find out who they belong to and get them back to their owners," Mrs. Surratt said.

"Well, now that poses a very interesting problem," Uncle Caleb continued. "You see, these are army horses. Union army horses."

Mrs. Surratt didn't hesitate at all before she said, "Then, I'll send my farmhand over to the post and tell the soldiers to come and get them."

"Do you really think that is the best idea?" Uncle Caleb asked.

"What else can we do?"

"Under the circumstances, I thought we might work out some sort of bargain," Uncle Caleb suggested.

"What kind of a bargain?" Tildy thought Mrs. Surratt sounded suspicious.

"These animals were caught trespassing on your land. They were destroying private property . . . your property. I feel like that entitles you to some sort of compensation."

Mrs. Surratt didn't say anything. She just stood quietly and looked at Uncle Caleb with a quizzical expression.

Uncle Caleb laid out his plan. "It took me and Lucius and Cato some time to get them under control so they wouldn't completely destroy your garden. I reckon we're entitled to a share of them, too. Supposing you keep three of them to cover your losses and I'll take two of them as my share?"

"Caleb Larrabie! I cannot believe what I heard you say," Mary Surratt said indignantly. "Neither one of us has any right to those horses. They belong to someone else."

"Not now they don't. Finders keepers. Bounty of war."

"What you are proposing is downright wrong," Mrs. Surratt insisted.

"I thought you were supposed to be a loyal Southerner," Uncle Caleb said.

"I am, through and through. I've got a son in the Confederate army."

"Then why make a fuss about taking those Union horses? Keeping them from the Yankees might be our way of making things easier for our boys. You might say that is an act of patriotism."

Mary Surratt shook her head angrily. "You might say that, but I think you are just salving your own conscience. Keeping those horses would be nothing but out-and-out horse stealing."

"No, it ain't. It's politics," Uncle Caleb said.

"That's not politics. It's a matter of what's right and wrong. I have to answer to God for my actions," Mary Surratt declared. "I thank you for helping me round them up, but I'm not going to be a party to dishonesty."

"Well, if you're so all-fired holy," Uncle Caleb said, "You can just keep 'em. But don't you be surprised when the Union army don't pay you for rounding them up or for your ruined garden."

"I will take care of those horses until they can be returned to their legal owners. I don't care about collecting any money. Even if they paid me, I wouldn't take Union army money."

Uncle Caleb turned and moved as though he were going to unlock the barn door where the horses had been corralled. "Maybe I ought to just let them go again," he said.

Mrs. Surratt stood her ground, staring at him without flinching. To Tildy's surprise, Uncle Caleb stepped back a few paces. Then, he turned and headed back across the field to his own place with Lucius and Cato following close on his heels.

Tildy tagged along at a distance, but she was close enough to hear Uncle Caleb muttering under his breath, "Fool woman. Crazy, church-going, praying woman."

The scene around the dinner table that evening was as unsociable as usual. Uncle Caleb was silent, obviously still angry about his run-in with Mrs. Surratt that afternoon. He attacked the food on his plate as though he had the offending woman under his knife and fork.

Lucius, on the other hand, sat listlessly. He seemed not interested in his meal at all. His eyes had a glazed look about them. Tildy thought he appeared to have sought refuge in some far away place that none of them could follow. He leaned his elbows dreamily on the table, holding a bite of food on his fork poised in mid-air.

"Lucius," Uncle Caleb snapped, startling Tildy so that she almost dropped her own fork. "Sit up and eat your dinner like respectable folks do."

Tildy asked to be excused from the table and went out the back door to sit on the porch. She took the small volume of English history that Papa used to read to her.

She opened it and spread it across her lap. She knew that the rest of the family would gather on the front porch, which Uncle Caleb referred to as the verandah. She preferred to be here where she could see the fields and the woods beyond. She also liked to hear the sound of Juno singing as she worked around the back part of the large house, clearing up the dinner things. In a little while, Linny came outside and sat down on the lowest step. The girl had finished putting Summy and the other three Larrabie boys to bed. Cato sat on the ground below the porch, leaning back on his haunches as he whittled at a hunk of wood. Tildy drew in a deep breath thinking this was the most peaceful time of the entire day.

Tildy looked down at her book. It would soon be too dark to read. It was then that she noticed Lucius. He had come around the side of the house and started off across the field. He was walking in the direction of the Surratt place.

"I thought my Uncle Caleb told Lucius he was not ever to go to Surratt's," Tildy said.

"That Lucius. He goes lots of places he's not supposed to be," Linny laughed. "That boy! He's one slippery eel, that one is."

Tildy turned back to her book. It really wasn't any of her business what her cousin did. If he got caught disobeying and got in trouble with his father; well, that was his own business.

Tildy read until it was so dark she could not see any longer. She sat quietly in the comforting darkness until the house seemed very quiet. Linny and Cato went off to bed. At last she got up and went inside. She climbed the two long flights of stairs up to the attic room that she shared with her mother and sisters. The rising heat grew more stifling as she went up.

Mother and Elizabeth and Louisa were already in bed. She could hear them breathing deeply. She marveled at their ability to sleep in the stuffy room.

Tildy got into her nightdress and lay on her cot, twisting and turning trying to find a cooler spot. After what seemed an hour or so, she got up and went to stand at the window. Perhaps she could get a breath of fresh air. She stood staring idly out at the darkness. Across the field she could see that there were still lights on over at the Surratt place. She supposed that wasn't out of the ordinary. Aunt Rachel had told her that people came and went at odd hours at a tavern where travelers stopped for overnight lodging.

Tildy started to go back to her cot when she noticed a single light bobbing up and down in the distance. It must be in the field. Someone was carrying a lantern and moving in this direction. The light came closer and then suddenly snuffed out.

Tildy recalled that Lucius had gone in the direction of Surratt's place after dinner. It was very late for him to be coming back home. He had probably doused his light when he got close to home so that his father wouldn't see it. She wondered what in the world he could possibly be doing over at Surratt's this time of night.

When Tildy finally was able to get to sleep, she slept deeply and long. When she awakened the next morning the sun was high in the sky and she was alone in the third floor room. She got up and dressed quickly and hurried downstairs. She found the entire household in a turmoil.

Only Mother and her sisters and the younger Larrabie children were at the breakfast table.

"Juno found Lucius unconscious early this morning," Roseanne announced. "He was lying on the ground out back."

"Uncle Caleb picked him up and carried him inside the house just as though he were a little baby," Elizabeth added. "I saw him do it."

Tildy had a hard time imagining Uncle Caleb doing such a tender thing.

"My father sent Cato to fetch the doctor," said Annabelle. "Lucius has probably got the malaria again."

"Probably he's got my laria," Louisa chimed in, not wanting to be left out of the excitement.

"Girls," Mother said. "You had better finish your breakfast now."

Tildy heard voices in the front entryway. She looked up and saw Uncle Caleb and Aunt Rachel accompanied by a tall man in a black suit. They were talking in hushed tones.

"I had hoped that he would escape the fever this year," Aunt Rachel said and Tildy could tell that her tone was worried.

"Once it gets into the blood, it's hard to get rid of," the doctor said. "Now, Mrs. Larrabie, I want to warn you about taking care of yourself. You must not let your concern for your son injure your own health. It could be bad for both you and your baby, particularly at this time."

For the next several days the entire Larrabie household revolved around the business of taking care of Lucius. Everyone tiptoed about and talked in whispers.

Despite the doctor's warning, Aunt Rachel insisted on being by her son's bedside constantly during the day. She sat bathing his fevered forehead and patting his pale hands.

To Tildy's great surprise, Uncle Caleb moved a small cot into Lucius' room. He spent every night there, keeping watch over the ailing boy.

Soon the doctor had to be called back to the Larrabie house. This time it was for Aunt Rachel. Despite everyone's efforts to prevent it, she had insisted on climbing the stairs to Lucius' second floor bedroom. She stayed up there the entire day. Juno brought her meals up on a tray. The strain and worry of taking care of Lucius had taken its toll on her, however. The new baby, which she had expected to arrive in mid-October, was born in late August.

Now, there were three invalids in the house. Lucius, Aunt Rachel, and the tiny, sickly, baby girl lay in three separate rooms.

Tildy saw that Uncle Caleb, himself, began to look like a ghost. He was paler and thinner than he had been before. He was up before first light each morning, trying to keep up with his farm work during the day. He spent most of the night watching over his wife and Lucius, moving about from one room to the other. Tildy wondered when he managed to sleep.

Juno took over care of the newest little Larrabie. Tildy thought it sad that the tiny girl had not even been given a name as yet, but no one seemed to have the time.

Linny took over full-time care of Summy and the three youngest Larrabie boys. Mother did the cooking and supervised Annabelle and Roseanne as well as her own two daughters. It wasn't until they were all in bed that Mother could find time to do her sewing. Tildy could see that Mother, too, was becoming quite weary from the extra burdens placed on her.

Even Cato was hard-pressed to keep up with the work load. He found himself having to do Lucius' work as well as his own. Tildy figured that was why he didn't object at all when she insisted on helping with the milking and some of the other farm chores. After the first day, Uncle Caleb himself seemed to accept having Tildy work right along beside him. Once in a while, he seemed to forget who she was and ordered her to do a task as though he had been talking to Cato or Lucius.

Tildy thought things would have been much easier still if Elizabeth and Annabelle and Roseanne had been pressed into service, too. She could name a dozen things those little girls could do to help out if they weren't so busy being such grand little ladies. Elizabeth had always helped gather eggs at home and do other chores. Tildy decided that she'd better not press her luck by suggesting such a thing to Uncle Caleb, however.

Mother was brave enough to confront Uncle Caleb, however. One evening after the children had all been fed, Mother marched boldly into Aunt Rachel's room. She confronted her brother-in-law as Tildy watched with admiration from the doorway.

"Caleb, you have got to consider yourself. What good will you be to your family if you keep up this pace and become ill yourself? Now, you go right downstairs and eat a decent dinner at the table."

"But, I was just going to help Rachel with her meal. She eats better when I'm here," he objected.

"I can do that," Mother said. "I'm sure Rachel will eat better if she knows that you are having a good meal."

Mother looked over at her sister. The frail woman in the bed managed to nod her head in a solemn promise.

"There's Lucius to be thought of," Caleb protested. "I still have to see that he gets fed."

"Tildy will help Lucius with his tray, won't you, Tildy?"

Tildy was too surprised to object. When Mother motioned in her direction, Tildy went obediently to Lucius' room. For the next thirty minutes, she pleaded and coaxed and did her best to get the invalid to swallow the nourishing chicken broth that she had brought upstairs for him.

Lucius was still so weak and feverish he could hardly keep his eyes open. Tildy guided the spoon to his mouth and talked to him the same way she would have talked to a baby.

When he kept dozing off, she would say, "Lucius, you've got to eat this good soup to get your strength back."

"I don't want it," Lucius whined.

"You can't get well if you won't eat."

"I don't want to eat," Lucius said. He closed his eyes and his head lolled back on his pillow.

"I don't care what you want to do," Tildy said in her firmest voice. "You've got to eat. It's an order."

"An order?" Lucius mumbled, his eyes flickering slightly. "An order? Whose order?"

Tildy said the first thing that popped into her head. "It's an order from Jefferson Davis . . . and from General Robert E. Lee."

At these words, Lucius' eyes opened a bit wider. He seemed to be staring right at Tildy but she wasn't sure he was seeing her at all. He appeared to be in that same faraway land he had been in that night at the dinner table. The night he had become ill.

"President Davis and General Lee want me to eat?" Lucius asked.

"Yes," Tildy said. She felt silly saying such things, but she wanted him to finish his soup so that she could have done with it and leave his room.

"I'll do anything to serve the Confederacy," Lucius said groggily.

"Then eat this," Tildy commanded. "You can't be a good Reb . . . Confederate soldier if you're sick in bed."

Dutifully Lucius gulped down a spoonful of soup.

Tildy wiped his chin as he said, "There are lots of ways to serve the South without being a soldier."

"That's right," Tildy agreed, offering another sip of the broth. "Lots of ways to serve."

"Like Johnny does. He's not a soldier like his brother, but his work is just as important."

Tildy had no idea what Lucius was babbling about, but as long as he continued to get the soup down, she was willing to go along with it. "Oh, yes. I'm sure Johnny's work is very, very important."

"Not everyone can be a spy," Lucius said, in between sips. "Not everyone can get messages through Northern lines."

"That's right," Tildy said, spooning up more soup to the delirious boy.

"Johnny is very brave," Lucius murmured. "He could get shot for what he's doing if he gets caught."

"Yes, yes," Tildy said, hardly listening. She was bored with the childish game by now.

"But when the men of the Northwest rise up and release the prisoners, we'll show the Yankees that we're not beat yet."

"Shhhh!" Tildy urged. "Just have this last spoonful of soup. Then you can rest."

"But, I've got to help Johnny," Lucius insisted. "When the prisoners are free. . . ."

"No more talking now," Tildy insisted. "Lie back and close your eyes like a good soldier and sleep."

"But, I've got to be ready," Lucius rambled on. "August 16. That's when it's going to happen. August 16."

Lucius seemed to grow more and more agitated. His talk was not making any sense at all. Tildy wished that she had not started this business about pretending to be soldiers. She was afraid she had made his condition worse.

"Lie back and close your eyes and try to rest," Tildy said. Then she added for good measure, "That is an order."

"An order?" Lucius asked.

"Yes, an order," Tildy said to the feverish boy.

Lucius sank back onto his pillow, exhausted. "Got to follow orders."

Frantically, Tildy soaked a cloth in the basin that was on the table beside his bed. She squeezed out the excess water and wiped it over his forehead.

"There now, that should feel better," she said.

Lucius nodded and soon was breathing deeply.

Tildy could not help but feel sorry for him. With a pang of conscience she recalled her hasty words to him the other day when she had been angry. She had told him that other boys his age were in the Confederate uniform. She should not have chided him that way about serving the cause he said he cared so much about. She realized now that there was no way that a boy who suffered as he did from recurrent bouts of malaria could ever hope to be a soldier. She felt ashamed of herself for teasing him. He was certainly not like those healthy sons of Mrs. Pettibone's back in Indiana. Those big strapping fellows had paid someone else to take their place in uniform so they could stay at home.

With one last look at Lucius, to make certain he was sleeping peacefully, Tildy tiptoed out of his room.

Life is certainly complicated and confusing sometimes, she thought. Lucius was sneaky, obnoxious, and boastful. She didn't like him very much. Yet, she felt sorry for him. She never could hold with slavery, yet she could understand that he was as devoted to his cause as she was to hers.

Then, there was Mary Surratt. Tildy liked the woman a lot. Tildy heard how Mary Surratt had fed Union soldiers. Tildy had seen with her own eyes that Mrs. Surratt would not keep Union army horses that did not belong to her. In fact, she had insisted that she would not even take any money for the damages those horses had done to her property. But it was this same Mary Surratt who had declared her loyalty to the South. She had a son in the Rebel army.

Finally, there was the puzzle of Uncle Caleb. He was grouchy and bossy and unpleasant to be around. On the other hand, he was gentle and kind to Aunt Rachel and Lucius. He was nearly wearing himself out tending to them. He really seemed to love them dearly. In fact, Tildy had seen him take that tiny little newborn baby of his from Juno's arms. Uncle Caleb had cradled that tiny bundle in his arms and even crooned a soft tune as he walked about the room trying to comfort the crying child.

Yes, life and people were indeed complicated and confusing.

It was not until Tildy lay in bed that night that she remembered some of the things Lucius had said in his delirium. Lucius had talked about Johnny being a spy. Could he have meant Johnny Surratt? Lucius had talked about prisoners being released. He had said that he must be ready to help when the prisoners were released on August 16. That didn't make sense at all. Or did it?

She remembered Lucius' earlier boast to her one day when they had been arguing. He had said that something important was going to happen. It would be something that would show the North that the South wasn't beaten yet. What if August 16 were the date he had been talking about? But, that didn't make any sense at all. August 16 had come and gone. It was now August 20.

Tildy shook her head. That was just Lucius' fever talking. Or was it?

118

9

Tildy had not planned to teach Cato and Linny to read. It had all come about so naturally that she was not really aware that she had become involved in schooling them.

It had started when she took her turn sitting with Lucius every afternoon. As much as she disliked her cousin, Tildy knew that helping to care for the recovering boy was something that everyone had to take a turn with.

Juno and Linny and Mother had their hands full trying to take care of the invalids in the Larrabie household. In addition, they had the usual routine of cooking and cleaning the large house and keeping the clothes washed up.

Juno, herself, sat day after day holding Aunt Rachel's tiny new baby. She sang and talked to the little girl by the hour. It was as though she was trying to transfer some of her own strength into the weak little body by the force of her love. The child lived almost three weeks after its early birth. When the baby's fretful crying stopped at last, Juno would allow no one but herself to prepare the child for burial. Then, Juno insisted on staying with Aunt Rachel, who was not strong enough to leave her bed to join the rest of the family as they walked slowly out to the family cemetery at the edge of the grove of trees.

Lucius, however, was getting better every day. At least, that is what Juno declared in disgust.

"When all a boy can do is fuss at folks who're trying to help him, he's about ready to get outta that bed and do for himself."

Tildy agreed heartily with that statement. She was tired of being her cousin's lackey. She was certain he took great delight in ordering her about to do this or that for him. Whenever she balked, he would pretend to have a sudden relapse. Although she was certain he was using his illness to take advantage of everyone, they wanted so much for him to get well, that they gave in and did exactly what he wanted them to do.

Tildy felt quite proud of herself, however, when she found a solution to her problem. It not only kept him from demanding that she do whatever he demanded, it was something that she liked to do for a couple of pleasant hours.

Tildy started reading out loud to Lucius each day from the *History of England* that had belonged to Papa. She found that she could lose herself in the story. It was almost possible to forget where she was and whom she was with.

She found herself looking forward to that time each day, especially when the doctor finally decreed that Lucius was well enough to go downstairs. The doctor thought it would be beneficial to him to take some fresh air before dinner. "It will stimulate his appetite."

Soon, Tildy noticed that Lucius was not the only person she was reading aloud to as they sat outside. Elizabeth and Louisa and Annabelle and Roseanne hovered about, each of them trying to get the closest place near Tildy's chair.

Before long, the group had increased in size as Linny brought the seven-year-old twins, Calhoun and Jefferson, outside. Linny sat on the step holding onto four-year-old Edmund while he played with his wooden horses. She held a squirming two-year-old Sumter on her lap. Tildy found that she took great pleasure in reading as dramatically as she could. She was surprised at how quiet the children, except for Summy, were during that story time.

Then, one day a new member was added to her audience. Late one afternoon when Mother rang the dinner bell, Cato and Uncle Caleb came up from the fields. As Cato waited his turn to splash his face at the pump, he moved closer to the porch and stood listening.

Tildy was certain by the look on his face that he was fascinated. He hardly moved when Uncle Caleb stamped his boots loudly on the porch. Cato seemed to forget about splashing his face as Uncle Caleb noisily used the metal scraper by the back door to clean the soil off his boots before he entered the house.

Uncle Caleb cleared his throat loudly and said, "Remember, you all have to be dressed for dinner."

Everyone chorused, "Yes, sir."

Uncle Caleb went inside, slamming the door behind him. Shortly he reappeared and said, "Cato. Get washed up and get inside."

Tildy knew by his lagging feet that Cato could hardly bear to leave his place on the porch.

To end his misery, Tildy closed the book and said, "You heard Uncle Caleb. We had better get ready for dinner."

Later that evening, after their meal, when the rest of the family had gathered in the parlor before dark, Tildy went out to the back verandah again. Cato was busy stacking wood in the box by the back door. It would be needed to start up the fire in the stove early the next morning for breakfast.

Although there was no one else around except the young black boy, Tildy started to read out loud. She read in a tone loud enough that she knew he would be able to hear as he worked.

When Cato finished his work, he took his usual place on the ground below the verandah, sitting on his haunches. He did not move as Tildy read until it grew too dark for her to see the words on the page any longer.

As she stood up to go inside the house, Tildy asked, "Did you like that story, Cato?"

"Like magic," Cato said.

"What do you mean?"

"You look at marks on that page and you know what words to say out loud. Like magic."

Tildy laughed and started to say, "It's only reading. Everybody does it," but she stopped short before uttering the words. Something in Cato's expression made her say instead, "In a way, you're right, Cato. I guess it is a kind of magic."

After that, it became part of the daily routine for Tildy to read to Cato on the back steps after dinner. Often she was joined by Linny after the girl had finished her task of putting the younger Larrabie boys to bed for the night.

One evening when Tildy read to them the story of Queen Matilda, Cato's eyes were shining. "That Matilda!" he said. "Her name's almost the same as yours."

Tildy was pleased that he had noticed the similarity.

"You're right," Tildy explained. "My father liked the story about this queen so much, he named me after her. People call me Tildy, but my full name is actually Matilda."

"Well, I reckon!" said Linny.

"You mean you got the same name as in that magic?" Cato asked.

"Yes," Tildy said. "Do you want to see it?"

For a moment, Cato hesitated as though he were afraid of the words on the page. Linny, however, leaned forward eagerly to look at the place where Tildy had put her finger under the name.

"Right there? That right there says Tildy?" Linny asked.

"It says Matilda," said Tildy.

Slowly Cato crept forward and leaned over to look at the page. Tildy could see that he was silently forming the word "Matilda" with his lips.

That evening when the household was quiet and she lay in bed, she thought about the look of wonder that she had seen on the faces of Linny and Cato when they had found the name "Matilda" on the page of the book. Tildy thought that Cato had been right. It was indeed magic. But, it was magic that everyone ought to be able to work. Tildy thought how lucky she was to be able to read. What pleasure it had brought to her. No one should have to go through life not knowing how to read. As she drifted off to sleep, an idea was beginning to take shape in Tildy's mind. She could hardly wait for the next day so that she could try it out.

That evening after dinner Tildy went out to sit on the back verandah as usual. This evening, however, she had not only her book with her. She had two pieces of paper. On each one of the pieces of paper, she had printed her name—M-A-T-I-L-D-A. She tried to make the letters just as they had appeared in the book. She handed one paper to Linny. The other she gave to Cato. Cato looked at it a bit suspiciously.

"That paper has my name on it," Tildy explained.

Then she opened the history book to the story of Queen Matilda.

"Now, look at the word on your paper," Tildy directed. "Then see if you can find a word that looks just like it on this page."

Cato squinted his eyes. He looked first at the paper he held in his hand and then at the words on the printed page in the book. Back and forth. Back and forth he looked from paper to book.

Tildy had just about given up hope that he could do it when he suddenly let out a shout, "There. Right there. Matilda!"

Tildy was so excited she could hardly speak. "You're right, Cato. You're right. You've found it."

"I see it, too," cried Linny, placing her finger on the correct place in the book.

Tildy couldn't remember when she had been more excited. She repeated this exercise each evening until both Cato and Linny could locate the name "Matilda" on the printed page without the help of the papers that she had made for them.

Tildy's next idea did not turn out so well. Thinking of the story about Queen Matilda and her loyal helpers,

Tildy printed the word K-N-I-G-H-T on a piece of paper. When she asked Cato and Linny if they knew what a "knight" was, each of them had the same answer. "It's when it gets dark out." Tildy could see that she had made a mistake. She realized that people need to understand what it is they are reading or it is just being able to recognize a word.

Tildy tried to think of a simple word that everyone used each day. She decided that the word "the," was the most common. What she hadn't counted on was the fact that both Cato and Linny pronounced it, "de."

And, to Tildy's surprised, neither one of them could tell her what it meant. She was even more surprised that she, herself, had such a hard time explaining it.

"It's a figure of speech. It's an article," she stammered, frustrated that they didn't know anymore about the word after she had finished explaining it. Teaching had turned out to be a lot more difficult than she had supposed it would be.

The words "and," "so," or "when" turned out to be equally impossible to use. They were too simple. She discarded the word "castle" because they had no experience with such a thing and couldn't even imagine it. It seemed that no words in the story really lent themselves to what she wanted to do. That first night when they had found the word "Matilda" on the page had made her think it would be easy to teach them the magic.

At last, Tildy selected the word, "man." Both Linny and Cato had no trouble telling her what a man was. In spite of this, neither could find it on the printed page, though they both tried very hard. Tildy decided that Matilda had been easier to locate among the many words because it was capitalized. She was afraid they would get discouraged. She did not know just how much patience they would have where "the magic" was concerned.

At last Tildy hit on what she thought was the perfect plan. She herself would write little stories about their everyday life. She would use words they were familiar with. The sentences would have to be short.

Tildy labored over her simple little stories, trying to get them just right. Finally she thought she had something she could use. She could hardly wait for that evening to try it out on them.

As Cato and Linny crowded close to her, she read aloud the words she had printed in large letters on a sheet of paper.

CATO AND LINNY LIVE AT CALEB LARRABIE'S HOUSE.
CATO HELPS IN THE FIELDS AND IN THE BARNS.
LINNY HELPS JUNO IN THE HOUSE.
LINNY ALSO TAKES CARE OF THE TWINS.

Cato and Linny sat absolutely still as Tildy read the story out loud. When she had finished, Cato shook his head in wonder.

Linny said softly, "The magic says that?"

Tildy nodded.

"The magic is about us?" Linny asked, her voice barely above a whisper. "It says Cato and Linny?"

"That's right," Tildy assured her.

"Say it out loud again," Linny insisted.

Tildy thought she would never get to their reading lesson that evening. Linny and Cato begged her to repeat the simple little story she had written about them over and over and over again.

She pointed to their own names, which she had printed on the paper. Each of them reached out and touched the names with a kind of reverence. Tildy knew she would never forget the looks on their faces as long as she lived. When it got too dark to continue, Tildy handed Linny the piece of paper with the story on it. Linny stood holding it in her hand as though she held a bag of gold.

After that, reading lessons got to be a regular thing each evening. Tildy found herself looking forward to that time each day. It gave her some purpose. It helped her get through the rest of the things she had to do. Now, when she helped Mother with her sewing or when she sat with Lucius, the reading lessons were always in the back of her mind.

One afternoon, Tildy and her mother sat sewing. Tildy was trying to be extremely careful with the fabric and the needle. She concentrated very hard on her stitches. It occurred to her that this must be what it was like for Linny and Cato to try to learn to read. They wanted more than anything else to do it. Maybe she could use their example to learn to sew as well as Mother. It had to be something you really wanted to do. She remembered how hard it had been to learn to plow. Papa used to tell her that she could learn to do anything if she would just put her mind to it. The only difference was that she had wanted to learn to plow. She had never wanted to learn to sew. Tildy knew how much Mother needed her help with the sewing now. She determined she would put her mind to this.

That afternoon, Mother said, "There now, I am almost finished with this petticoat for Mrs. Surratt. All I have to do is to take it over to her house and see if she likes the lace I plan to trim it with."

"Why not let me do that for you?" Tildy offered, thinking it would be a good excuse to get out of the house for a while. "Lucius dropped off to sleep almost as soon as I started reading to him, so he doesn't need me. Maybe you could rest a bit while I run this errand for you."

"I suppose there is really no need for me to go," Mother said. "Mrs. Surratt can look at the lace sample and see if it is what she wants me to put on the petticoat."

"Then you must stay here," Tildy insisted. "Lie back awhile and close your eyes. I'll pull the draperies."

"You're right, Tildy," Mother said. "I really am very tired. It would be a great help to me for you to do this."

Tildy looked at her mother's face. The strain of the last few months showed plainly. Tildy made up her mind that she was going to try very hard to help Mother and not to cause her any worries.

Tildy went outside and across the field to the Surratt house. She breathed deeply as she walked. It was good to be able to get out-of-doors like this.

When Tildy reached the Surratt place, she had just stepped up onto the porch and raised her hand to knock when the door suddenly swung open. Three rough-looking men came outside. Their heavy boots clomped noisily on the wooden porch. They walked past her, not even tipping their hats when they saw her as any gentleman would normally do. Tildy stepped back and looked at them with distaste.

She supposed that this is what it was like running a tavern. People came and went at all hours. You hadn't much control over what kind of persons they were. Tildy could certainly understand why Mrs. Surratt was eager to leave here and move to the city. Although Tildy's recollection of that place was that it was also crowded with people of every sort. She supposed Mrs. Surratt would be able to choose whom she rented her rooms to if she ran a boardinghouse rather than a way station.

Tildy turned to watch the men as they mounted their horses and rode away. When they were gone, Tildy knocked on the door and Anna answered it.

"Why Matilda, what a pleasant surprise," Anna greeted her. "Do come inside. What brings you here?"

"I have some petticoats that Mother has finished except for the lace. She wants to get your mother's approval before she sews it on."

Anna led Tildy to the parlor. "You wait here. I'll go and bring my mother to you."

As Tildy waited, she wandered about the parlor, looking at Mrs. Surratt's furnishings. There was a pretty little writing desk decorated with painted flowers. There was also a nice three legged table. Tildy ran her hand over the smooth wood. Mrs. Surratt had some nice things but they couldn't compete with the things in the Larrabie's fancy parlor.

From the rooms across the hall, Tildy could hear the sound of voices coming from the room where the post office was, with the tavern beyond. Her curiosity was aroused. She walked to the parlor door to get a better view. She looked and then looked again to make certain she hadn't been mistaken. She had thought she saw someone crouching behind the work counter. She stepped closer to the door to get a clearer look. She was right. There was someone hiding back there. And, that someone was very familiar. Although she couldn't see the face and the figure was doubled over, she thought it appeared to be Lucius!

How could that be? He was back at home, asleep in his own bed. Tildy had made sure of that before she left him earlier this afternoon. Still, it looked very much like Lucius. Before Tildy could move closer so that she could see better, Mrs. Surratt came hurrying along the hallway, her dark skirts rustling as she moved.

"Matilda, my dear," Mrs. Surratt said in her soft welcoming voice. "I didn't mean to keep you waiting so long. I had some business to attend to at the back of the house."

"That's all right," Tildy said. "I didn't mind waiting." As Mrs. Surratt led the way into the parlor, Tildy tried to peer over Mrs. Surratt's shoulder for one last look at whoever it was who was hiding in the other room, but Mrs. Surratt was too tall and Tildy could not see.

"Mother wanted your approval of this lace before she stitched it in place," Tildy said, hoping this would not take long. Tildy wanted to hurry back to the Larrabie place as fast as possible. She wanted to find out if Lucius were still asleep. Surely he would not be over here at Surratt's. And, even if he were, why would he be hiding that way?

"Oh, this does look lovely," Mrs. Surratt said. She moved over to the window, carrying the petticoat so that she could inspect it more closely in the bright light. She pulled back the heavy lace curtains and held it up near the glass. "Oh, yes, just lovely. This lace will be fine. Your mother has such good judgment. And, I don't think I have ever seen such tiny, neat stitching."

"Thank you," Tildy said. "My mother will be pleased that you like her work."

"Now, my dear, shall I have Anna bring us some refreshment?"

Ordinarily Tildy would have relished the opportunity for a visit with Mrs. Surratt. Right now, however, she was eager to get back across the fields and check on Lucius.

"Thank you, but I can't stay for refreshments," Tildy said regretfully. "I must hurry back. There is ever so much to be done."

"I understand," Mrs. Surratt said, walking with Tildy to the door.

Tildy had hoped for one more glance through the open doorway across from the parlor, but Mrs. Surratt had walked between her and that room.

Once outside the house and as soon as she was certain that Mrs. Surratt was no longer watching her departure, Tildy broke into a gallop. Across the field she went, her long skirts whipping about her legs. Then, she tripped and fell flat in the dirt. As she got up, Tildy discovered that she had fallen right on top of the newly stitched petticoat that Mother had made for Mrs. Surratt. Frantically she tried to dust the mustard-colored dust from the snowy white fabric.

"Oh no," Tildy cried. "Whatever will Mother say when she sees this? After I had made up my mind to try so hard not to cause Mother any more worries, how could I have done this?"

Tildy got up and hurried back to the house. She peeked into the parlor. She was relieved to see that Mother was still resting on the small brocade love seat. Her eyes were closed and her breathing was deep.

Tildy rushed upstairs to Lucius' room. She pushed the door open quietly. Lucius was lying in bed just as she had left him. He, too, was sleeping soundly, the covers pulled up securely under his chin.

Tildy tiptoed closer to look at him. She had been so certain that he was the person she had seen hiding behind the counter in the post office in Surratt's house. But, Lucius lay, eyes closed. He breathed deeply the way he had slept when the terrible fever was on him, droplets of sweat forming a pattern on his forehead and his upper lip and across the bridge of his nose.

Tildy went down the back stairway to the kitchen at the rear to find Juno. Maybe Juno would be able to help her get the dirt off the petticoat before Mother awakened.

Juno was standing at the floury kitchen table, punching down the yeast dough that had risen in a large crockery bowl. The black woman looked up when she saw Tildy, "Land's sake, child. What have you been doing? Just look at your face."

Tildy put her hand up to wipe her face and realized that her forehead and the bridge of her nose and her upper lip were covered with droplets of perspiration . . . just as Lucius' had been.

"I was running across the fields," Tildy explained. Although she knew she wouldn't be able to prove a thing, she was almost certain that Lucius had done exactly as she had. He had beaten her back to the house by running across the field. That explained why he was so sweaty. It wasn't the fever at all. He was only pretending to be asleep. As Tildy thought back on it now, it seemed strange that he would have had the covers so snugly under his chin when he was perspiring so. She guessed that under the covers Lucius was fully dressed. He was only pretending to be asleep.

Before dinner that afternoon Tildy read aloud to Lucius on the verandah as she had on other afternoons. She debated whether or not she should say anything to him about the escapades of today. She had heard Uncle Caleb tell him on more than one occasion that he was to stay away from Surratt's. Why had he been over there today and what was it he was hiding from?

"Well?" Lucius asked.

"Well, what?" Tildy replied.

"Why did you stop reading all of a sudden?" he wanted to know.

"I was just thinking about something," she said.

"Were you thinking about how you are teaching Linny and Cato to read?" Lucius asked.

Tildy looked at her cousin in surprise. "How did you know about that?" she asked.

"I know a lot of things," Lucius said in a tone of voice that Tildy thought sounded very smug.

She wondered how he had found out about the evening reading lessons on the back verandah. He was supposed to have gone right to bed immediately after supper each night. Tildy guessed that he must have sneaked down the back stairway and listened at the rear door. Now, she was more certain than ever that it had been Lucius she had seen hiding over at Surratt's. It would not be the first time Tildy had caught him eavesdropping.

"Yes, I have been teaching Linny and Cato to read," she said defiantly. "What's wrong with that?"

"I'll tell you what's wrong." Tildy thought Lucius' eyes had a triumphant glint about them as he spoke. "Teaching slaves to read is against the law. That's what's wrong."

"I don't believe you," Tildy said.

"You had better believe me," he said. "But, I won't tell anybody. We'll let it be our little secret for now. That is, if you are good at keeping secrets."

Lucius glared at Tildy, his eyes a hard steely color. Although he hadn't come right out and said it in so many words, Tildy had a feeling that he was warning her that she had better keep his secret, too. He must know he had been caught over at Surratt's. He was trading her secret for his.

10

It was early in October that Uncle Caleb learned that even though Tildy was a girl, she could be a very real help to him. As it turned out, Uncle Caleb was not the only one who learned something surprising from the experience.

It all started with another dispute at the Larrabie meal table.

Ordinarily Tildy would not have been present when it happened. She had discovered that Uncle Caleb got up each morning at dawn and worked outside for a few hours while it was still cool before coming into the house for his breakfast. Tildy usually managed to go downstairs to eat her morning meal while he was busy outside. That way she could be gone before he appeared at the table. But this morning was the first time that Aunt Rachel had felt well enough to come to the dining room to eat. Tildy and Mother had lingered over their meal in order to sit with Aunt Rachel and encourage her to eat a nourishing breakfast.

"At this rate," Mother said to her sister, "We shall see roses blooming in your cheeks again. Do have another buckwheat cake."

"I think I will," Aunt Rachel said, taking the plate Mother had handed her. "And, I think that I feel well enough to take a bit of a stroll this morning."

Tildy thought things were going rather well until Uncle Caleb came into the room and said, "Lucius, I want you to drive the wagon down to Port Tobacco tomorrow and pick up some casks."

Aunt Rachel stopped eating and said, "Oh, Caleb, the boy is simply not well enough yet to do such a thing."

"Well, what am I going to do?" Uncle Caleb wanted to know. "I must have those casks. I've got to send somebody down there but I can't go after them. I can't spare Cato either. He's doing Lucius' work as well as his own."

"I can go, Mother," Lucius insisted. "Really, I am well enough for that."

"You're still weak," Aunt Rachel said, reaching over to pat her son's hand. "A trip such as that would take the entire day. You would wear yourself out and be ill again."

"But, Mother," Lucius pleaded. "I've been counting on it. I always go for the casks. I can do it. Please, you've got to let me go."

Tildy was more than a bit puzzled at what she was hearing. Could Lucius actually be begging to be allowed to do something that sounded like work? Usually, he spent most of his energy trying to get out of jobs that needed doing.

"I can't see the harm that could come of it," Uncle Caleb said.

"Handling those two horses and a wagon loaded with heavy casks requires a great deal of strength," Aunt Rachel said. "Lucius is simply not strong enough yet to exert himself that way. And you know that the doctor said he is to take a rest each day."

Uncle Caleb sighed and shook his head. "What am I going to do then?"

Tildy was pleased to see that Aunt Rachel was able to stand up to her domineering husband.

"Are you sure you can't send Cato?" Aunt Rachel asked.

"There's no way I could trust that boy by himself. Besides, I can't spare him here. We're busy staking the leaves."

"Oh, dear," Aunt Rachel's lower lip began to tremble and her hands shook so hard that she put her fork down on her plate with a clatter. Tildy thought her aunt was going to give in. She looked about ready to cry.

Uncle Caleb came over and put his rough hands on her shoulders. "There now, don't get yourself upset. I'll think of something. Maybe I can hire the Surratt's farmhand."

Tildy couldn't help thinking that the morning had been full of surprises. Uncle Caleb was usually so gruff, but he seemed kind and gentle when it came to Aunt Rachel. He actually seemed to care about his wife. He had even offered to hire someone to make the trip. Tildy remembered what Mother had told her about Uncle Caleb always being in debt. All of this gave Tildy the courage to make a suggestion.

"I could drive the wagon down to Port Tobacco to get the casks for you," Tildy said, attempting to sound as though she didn't care one way or another.

Perhaps she had sounded too indifferent. Uncle Caleb had not even responded to her offer. Perhaps he had not heard her. She repeated her idea, this time a bit louder than before.

Uncle Caleb's mood swung quickly back to that of his usual impatient gruffness. "Don't bother me with such foolishness right now. Can't you see that I have a problem?"

"It's not foolishness," Tildy insisted. "I can handle a team of horses. Don't you remember that I drove the wagon to Surrattsville from Washington on the day we arrived here?"

Uncle Caleb looked at Tildy as though he had just bitten into something very sour. "Indeed, I do remember that day very well. It gave everyone in the neighborhood something to talk about for a long time. I'm not about to provide them with another such spectacle."

"But you said you needed someone to . . . ."

Uncle Caleb's fist slammed down on the table, rattling the dishes and silverware. "Enough of this talk! I will not be made a laughingstock in this town by having a young girl in my household do menial labor."

Tildy started to open her mouth again when she felt Mother's hand pat her knee gently and saw Mother shake her head ever so slightly.

The room was quiet for a moment. All that could be heard was the sound of Uncle Caleb's spoon against the bowl as he dipped up the gruel he was eating.

"Caleb," Mother said very calmly. "I think perhaps Matilda has offered you the perfect solution to your problem. You have to have the casks. Someone has to go to get them. You can't go. You can't send Cato. Tildy is right about being a good teamster. Her father taught her well. Now, the way I see it, it would be no reflection on your family if I let her drive the wagon. She's a Graham, not a Larrabie. All the neighborhood knows that. If anyone criticizes, let the criticism be on me."

For a very long time Uncle Caleb did not reply. The sound of the clock ticking in the hallway measured every second. Tildy was afraid to look up. She kept her eyes carefully focused on her plate.

"She wouldn't know how to get there," Uncle Caleb said.

"Lucius could ride along with her," Mother said and then turned to Aunt Rachel. "If he didn't have to exert himself handling the horses, it wouldn't take any energy. He would go along merely to give Tildy directions."

Aunt Rachel looked at Lucius anxiously. "Well, I don't know . . . ."

Mother continued to talk in that reasonable tone of voice that Tildy knew so well. Papa had always said that Mother could charm a hen right off its nest.

"In fact, the fresh air might do Lucius a world of good. It has been quite pleasant the last few days, not anywhere near as hot as it was, and . . . " Mother added, "We could even make a pallet of quilts in the back of the wagon. Lucius could lie down on them and rest if he feels tired."

Tildy thought Lucius was about to say something, but Mother favored him with one of her firm glances and he sat quietly with his mouth gaping open.

More silence followed while Uncle Caleb and Aunt Rachel considered all that Mother had said. While they waited, Tildy picked up a biscuit from her plate and very deliberately and slowly spread butter on it. She was determined not to give Uncle Caleb the satisfaction of thinking that she cared one way or another what he finally decided.

With a quick movement, Uncle Caleb shoved his chair back. Tildy jumped as the legs screeched on the polished wooden floor. Without a word, he started to walk from the dining room. Then, he cleared his throat, turned back and glared directly at Tildy.

"Can you be ready to leave tomorrow morning, bright and early?"

Tildy gulped. It was impossible for her to keep pretending that she didn't care. She tried to speak but no words would come, so she just nodded her head.

All Tildy could think about the rest of that day was the trip she would be taking to Port Tobacco tomorrow. It seemed a great adventure to her. She would be proving to Uncle Caleb that she was strong and capable, that girls could do more than just sit around and wear fancy dresses to make them look pretty.

Sleep didn't come easily for Tildy that night and the next morning she was up and dressed while it was still dark. She went downstairs even before Juno had started the fire in the big stove in the kitchen to bake the bread.

"Well, I never thought to see you up at this hour," Juno said when she saw Tildy. "I expect you're raring to go."

"Can I help you with breakfast?" Tildy asked, not wanted to admit, even to Juno, how excited she was.

"If you want to be helping you can fix a lunch basket for you young'uns to take with you today."

140

Everyone else in the household seemed to have caught Tildy's spirit of anticipation. Everyone in the Larrabie and Graham families was up and ready by the time breakfast was on the table.

After eating, everyone walked out to make sure the wagon was ready. Aunt Rachel directed as Linny made a pallet of quilts in the back for Lucius. Juno stowed the lunch basket carefully under the high seat.

"Take me with you, Tildy," Louisa begged. "I'll be good and do what you tell me to do."

Tildy scooped her little sister up in her arms and hugged her. "I'm sure you would be a good girl, but I can't take you this time. Maybe next time." Tildy dared not glance at Uncle Caleb to see if he heard or reacted to the idea that there would be another such occasion.

Tildy kissed Louisa and put her into Mother's arms. Then Tildy climbed up on the wagon seat and took the reins in her hands. She sat for a moment, savoring the feel of the wide leather straps. She hoped no one noticed that she was a bit shaky as she wrapped them firmly about her hands.

"Now, you be careful," Mother said, not seeming to notice that the same words had been spoken by Aunt Rachel and Uncle Caleb and even Juno.

Once more Tildy repeated her solemn promise that she would be careful and that everything would be just fine.

Lucius got up on the seat beside her and sighed loudly.

"Lucius, you rest if you get tired. You hear?" Aunt Rachel reminded.

141

Lucius nodded his head dutifully and mumbled, "Yes, Mother."

Tildy made a clicking sound with her tongue and gently flicked the reins on the horses' flanks. The horses strained and the wagon wheels made a grinding sound.

"The brake lever," Uncle Caleb shouted. "The brake lever. You forgot to release the brakes."

Tildy's face burned with embarrassment as she realized that she had forgotten to do that.

It took all of Tildy's strength to pull up on the lever and Uncle Caleb didn't help any by muttering to himself in disgust about "sending a child to do a man's work."

At last they were on their way, rolling out of the barnyard and into the lane. Lucius had turned on the seat and was looking back and waving at the family. Tildy had all she could do to handle the team of horses. She knew they were getting used to her touch just as she was getting used to the way they pulled together.

When they reached the end of the long lane that led from the Larrabie house to the road, Lucius said, "Stop the wagon."

"What for?" Tildy wanted to know. She pulled up on the reins, wondering what was wrong. They had only gotten as far as the gate.

"I am going to drive the team the rest of the way," he said.

"Lucius, you must be crazy," Tildy said, irritated that he had called a halt just when she was getting the feel of the team. "You know what your mother said."

"I know what she said, but they've all gone inside the house. No one can see us now. I am going to drive from this point on."

Lucius spoke in such a commanding manner that Tildy almost gave in to him. She was already a little upset from the bad start when she had forgotten the brake handle.

Lucius reached over and tried to pull the reins from her hands, but the lines were wrapped securely, as Papa had taught her. The minute he started to pull, she held on as tightly as she could.

"If you think I am going to ride down the road and let everyone see a girl driving me in this wagon, then you've got another think coming."

"If you take these reins," Tildy said, very deliberately trying to keep her voice from showing how unnerved she was, "I will get out of this wagon. I will walk back to the house and tell them what you did."

Lucius glared at her. "You tell on me and I'll tell on you," he threatened.

"Just what do you think you can tell on me?" Tildy said, still hanging onto the reins.

"I'll tell my father that you are teaching Linny and Cato to read," he said. "I told you that was against the law."

"I don't believe you," Tildy insisted aloud, but inside she wasn't really sure whether Lucius was telling her the truth or not.

"You'll find out it is the law if you don't let me drive," Lucius said.

"Well, if it is a law, it shouldn't be and it won't be much longer," Tildy continued, sounding much braver than she felt. "The war is almost over. You know that General Grant is right outside of Richmond. When the

143

Southern capital falls there will be no more slavery anywhere."

Lucius' face turned very red and he loosened his grip on the reins for a moment. "The war isn't over yet. The North isn't going to win. Things are planned that will surprise you and all the Yankees."

Tildy laughed at Lucius' blustering. "You are always so full of talk," she said. "I've heard you bragging before about how there are plans and things are going to change, but nothing ever comes of all your talk."

"This time is different," Lucius said. "I know it for a fact."

"Stop trying to act so important," Tildy said, feeling sure he was bluffing. She just wanted to get moving again. "It's all wishful thinking. You don't really know anything about any plans."

"Oh, don't I?" Lucius would not give in. "You just wait and see. This time it's going to happen."

Beads of perspiration broke out on Lucius' forehead. Tildy hoped that this excitement was not going to make him ill again. She wished she had never challenged his word in the first place.

Tildy sighed. "Let's stop this, Lucius. It isn't getting us anywhere. You know that I am supposed to drive the team, but it's still very early in the morning. None of your neighbors are going to see you riding beside me on the wagon."

"But someone in Port Tobacco might see us," Lucius said sullenly. "I know lots of people there and I don't want to be driven by a girl through that town either."

144

"I'll tell you what," Tildy said. "When we get to Port Tobacco, I will let you drive while we are in town, but that is all. I drive the rest of the way as we promised your mother and mine."

Lucius was breathing hard. Tidly could see that their struggle had worn him out.

"All right," he agreed finally. "But, don't you change your mind. You've got to promise I can drive in Port Tobacco."

"I promise," Tildy said.

Once more, she snapped the reins and the team and wagon moved slowly forward with Tildy in charge.

"Why don't you lie down on the pallet in back?" Tildy suggested. "You look tired."

"I'm all right," Lucius sounded very angry.

Tildy was sorry she had said anything about him lying down. She knew he must think she was just gloating over having won the argument.

They rode for a long time without speaking to each other except when Lucius told Tildy which way to turn or which road to take. He seemed to be deep in thought. In a way, she felt sorry for her cousin. He was always making such wild claims about how the South had some secret plan that would surprise everyone. Yet, nothing ever came of it.

Tildy wasn't certain how far they had come, but it must have been a few miles outside of Surrattsville that they passed through a village called Camp Springs. Tildy noticed that there were many soldiers in blue uniforms in evidence here.

Lucius must have noticed her interest in them for he said, "I told you it was not going to be easy for the Yankees. Maryland may be a part of the Union, but the folks around here are for the South. They know it up in Washington, too. That's why there are so many soldiers around here."

Tildy thought it best that she not say anything. She didn't want to get the debate going between them again. She just wanted to ride and enjoy the day. Besides, seeing all those Union soldiers had made her think of Papa and she didn't feel much like talking about things that reminded her of the war and the fact that Papa would not be coming back.

Lucius seemed to be baiting her, however. "Old Abe isn't very popular in these parts. Did you know he only got one vote in this entire county in the last election?"

Tildy hadn't known that but would never give Lucius the satisfaction of admitting it. She held firmly to the reins and kept her eyes straight ahead, not saying a word.

"There's lots of folks who are helping the cause of the South," Lucius went on at length. She had a feeling he was enjoying himself at her expense now. "You'd be surprised if you knew how many are sympathetic to the South. Not all of them live in the South either. The day will come when everybody will find out how many people are on the side of the Confederacy." Lucius patted the pocket of his jacket with his hand. "Some things are going to become mighty plain before long. Then, no matter how many Union soldiers the Yankee generals send down here, it won't make any difference."

Tildy maintained her silence and before long Lucius quit talking and sat quietly as they rode along.

They stopped for lunch when the sun was high in the sky. Both of them ate ravenously from the basket of goodies that Tildy, with Juno's help, had packed earlier that morning. Tildy supposed it was the fresh air with a hint of autumn briskness that made them so hungry. Lucius leaned back against a tree and closed his eyes. Tildy let him sleep for a while. It gave her a chance to walk about by herself, enjoying the beauty of the countryside. They were in a long valley surrounded on either side by wooded hills. It wasn't at all like Indiana but Tildy had to admit that it was lovely. Suddenly, Tildy heard something moving behind her. She turned around quickly to see Lucius getting up and heading for the wagon.

She turned and ran back as fast as she could. Quickly she clambered up on the wagon seat and grabbed the reins before Lucius could get there. She knew he was only pretending to be asleep so that he could drive the wagon. Well, his trick had almost worked.

"Get the picnic basket," Tildy said. "It wouldn't do to leave it at the side of the road."

Unhappily Lucius turned back to do as she said. When he climbed back up on the wagon seat beside her, he pleaded, "Let me drive the rest of the way."

"I promised you that I would let you drive when we got to Port Tobacco," Tildy reminded him.

"We're almost there," Lucius said.

"I can't even see the town yet," Tildy said. "When we get closer, I will let you drive."

"Look," Lucius said, pointing straight ahead. "Here comes a buggy. I think it's someone I know. Let me hold the lines."

147

"Lucius, how could you possibly know who's in that buggy?"

"I come down here a lot and sometimes these people travel up to Washington. They stop over at Surratt's Inn. I see them there. I do know that buggy. See the rose-colored fringe around the top of the cab?"

Tildy sighed and wrapped the reins around the post. "We'll just sit here until that buggy passes. No one will know I have been the one driving."

The buggy slowed as it drew near them. Tildy saw that the fine rig was driven by a black man in a fancy suit. He wore a tall silk hat.

"Miss Floyd," Lucius called out. Quickly he jumped down from his seat on the wagon. "Miss Floyd."

Lucius ran to the center of the road. Tildy thought for a moment that the horse hitched to the buggy was going to run him down. The driver pulled up frantically on the lines and Tildy heard him shout, "What are you doing? Are you plumb crazy? Get out of the road."

Lucius seemed completely undisturbed that he had caused such commotion. "Miss Floyd, I am at your service." He took off his hat politely and bowed deeply from the waist.

Tildy could not believe what she was seeing. She thought people acted that way only in the books she read.

"Why, if it isn't young Master Larrabie," said a woman's voice, from the buggy. "You gave us quite a start, lad."

"It's a beautiful day for a drive, ma'am," Lucius continued.

148

"Indeed, it is a beautiful day," the woman had leaned forward so that Tildy was able to get a good look at her. She was exquisitely dressed. "And, is it a drive on a lovely autumn day that brings you to our part of the county? Or, are you on a secret mission?"

Tildy was certain she detected a tone of amusement in the woman's voice.

"No, ma'am," Lucius said seriously. "I am on an important errand for my father."

"To be sure," Miss Floyd said, nodding her head in exaggerated understanding.

"But, who knows what might happen when I reach Port Tobacco," Lucius continued importantly.

"Oh, I agree," Miss Floyd said. "One never knows when the opportunity to serve the cause will arise. True patriots must be ready to seize any opportunity."

Tildy saw the woman put her fan up in front of her lips to cover a smile, but the woman could not hide the merriment that glistened in her eyes. "There might even be contraband to smuggle out in the floorboard of the wagon."

Lucius turned to glance back at Tildy who was still sitting on the seat of the wagon. He lowered his voice to a conspiratorial tone. "We must be careful what we say. One never knows who is listening."

Quickly the woman put one gloved hand up to her mouth in mock horror. "You are absolutely right. Caution is our watchword."

Tildy realized with embarrassment that the woman was teasing Lucius. Even the man who drove the buggy was amused and had to turn his head away to keep from revealing his laughter at Lucius' expense. Lucius, himself, seemed not to notice that he was the object of their merriment.

"Who is the lovely young lady you have with you, Master Larrabie?" The woman seemed ready to change the subject.

"She's no young lady," Lucius said. "She's only my cousin."

"Well now, I remember once when I was about your age. I was quite taken with one of my cousins. He was a charming lad," the woman sighed at her own memory. "But, alas. It was never to be. The future had something else in store for me." The woman turned from Lucius and looked over at Tildy. "Would you like for me to tell your fortune, my dear? Are you interested in what the future holds in store for you?"

"I don't think she wants to know the future," Lucius said. "She's a Yankee."

"And you, my dear young man, are a Southerner," the woman said abruptly, "And southern gentlemen are always gallant toward any lady. I am sure I need not have to remind you of that."

Lucius seemed a bit chastised by her words. "Yes, ma'am."

"And a gentleman always introduces ladies when they meet."

"Yes, ma'am," Lucius bowed his ridiculous bow once more. "Miss Floyd, this is my cousin from Indiana, Miss Matilda Graham. Miss Graham, may I present Miss Olivia Floyd of Rose Hill."

Lucius had emphasized the words, "Rose Hill," as though it was very special. It meant nothing to Tildy.

"I'm pleased to meet you, Miss Floyd," Tildy said politely.

"And I am delighted to make your acquaintance, my dear," Miss Floyd said. "I do regret that I am not going to be at home today so that you could call on me. Next time, however, when you are in this part of the county, you must come to Rose Hill and join me for tea."

When Miss Floyd's buggy had at last driven away, Tildy asked. "What is Rose Hill and who is Miss Floyd? She seems to be quite a grand lady."

"She's much more than that," Lucius said. "And, Rose Hill is a noted plantation in these parts. Everyone knows Miss Floyd."

Before Tildy realized what had happened, Lucius had grabbed the reins, unwrapping them from the post. "Now, I will drive the rest of the way to Port Tobacco." He looked quite pleased with himself.

Tildy put her hands in her lap with a sigh of resignation. She contented herself with gazing about and enjoying the beautiful countryside.

Port Tobacco was a busy little town built around a square. There was a courthouse and hotels and a store. There were several nice looking houses. Lucius turned the horses down a side road to a place where he said they were to get the casks. Lucius stopped the wagon in front of a large warehouse and wrapped the reins on his side of the wagon. He looked at her in a challenging fashion. Tildy took a deep breath. Lucius did have a way of wearing a person down.

Lucius jumped down to the ground and said, "I'll go inside and make arrangements for the casks to be loaded on the wagon."

Tildy decided it would be best for her to wait at the wagon. After a few minutes Lucius came outside the warehouse, but he didn't get back up on the wagon seat. He seemed to be looking for something or someone. Suddenly Lucius called out and waved. Tildy was surprised when a rough-appearing man approached them. There was something about the man that made Tildy uneasy. Perhaps it was the way he was dressed. He had on a worn jacket and a dark shapeless hat. Perhaps it was the stubble on his chin or the way his small eyes darted back and forth. She shivered when he stared up at her curiously. It reminded her of the way she had felt that day she had encountered those men coming from Surratt's Inn.

"That's my cousin from Indiana," Lucius said, as though he wanted to dismiss her as quickly as possible and get on to more important things.

Tildy would have been glad not to be involved in this conversation at all. She looked away and started to scoot to the far side of the wagon seat, but not before she heard the man say, "Indiana, huh? Is she one of them Nu-Oh-Lac's?"

Lucius laughed. "Not her. She's a Yankee through and through."

Miss Floyd's lecture reminding Lucius that he was a southern gentleman seemed to have been completely forgotten.

Lucius took something from inside his coat pocket. Tildy could see that it was a small newspaper. Lucius handed it to the man and pointed at one of the printed articles in the paper.

The man took the paper and read the article. Tildy heard him exclaim, "Arrested, eh? So, that's why nothing came of it."

Lucius nodded.

"We didn't need them anyway."

The man started to say something else, but Lucius nudged him. The two of them walked a short distance away before they continued talking. Tildy could not hear anything else they said.

It wasn't until they were on their way back to Surrattsville once more that Tildy realized what word the man in Port Tobacco had used when asking about her. At first she hadn't really understood it clearly, the man had spoken with a bit of an accent.

"Nu-Oh-Lac," Tildy repeated to herself trying to make sure she had heard it correctly. It was a strange word but she felt certain that she had heard it somewhere before. "Nu-Oh-Lac," she whispered once more.

"What did you say?" Lucius asked.

"Oh, it was nothing," Tildy said. "I was just thinking about something."

It wasn't until late that night that Tildy remembered where she had heard that word before and found out what it meant.

11

It was long after the usual supper hour when Tildy and Lucius arrived back at the Larrabie house in Surrattsville. Tildy could see Mother and Aunt Rachel waiting out on the front verandah as the wagon rolled up the long lane leading to the house.

The two women hurried out to meet them. Tildy could tell from their manner that both of them were mightily relieved to see that Tildy and Lucius had arrived safely.

"Juno has kept your meal warm for you," Mother said. "She'll have it on the table as soon as you wash up."

Cato had been watching, too, from a perch on the fence. He had jumped down and run to spread the news. Uncle Caleb came out and climbed up on the wagon. "I'll take it on around to the back. Cato can help me unload the casks and put them in the shed."

Tildy supposed it was too much to expect Uncle Caleb to have thanked her for her help in making the trip to Port Tobacco.

Aunt Rachel hovered anxiously around Lucius, "Would you rather have your meal brought to your room on a tray? Did you rest at all during the trip? How do you feel? Are you sure you're all right? Do you have a fever?"

"I'm just fine," Lucius insisted. "I can eat at the table."

They all went into the dining room where Juno was busily laying out a spread for them.

As Tildy and Lucius ate, Mother and Aunt Rachel asked to hear all about their trip.

"Did you have any trouble handling the horses?" Mother wanted to know.

Tildy assured her that everything had been fine. She didn't volunteer that the only trouble she couldn't handle had been with Lucius who insisted on driving. He had driven almost all the way back home again, turning the reins over to her only when they were in sight of the Larrabie house. To get away from that ticklish subject, Tildy said, "We met a very interesting lady today."

Lucius made a strange strangled sound and seemed to choke on his soup.

Aunt Rachel jumped up from her place and hurried over to her son. "Are you certain you're all right, Lucius?"

"I'm fine," he said.

Tildy was sure he had given her a warning look. Somehow he didn't seem to want her to talk about their having encountered Miss Floyd on the road.

When calm was restored once more, Mother asked, "What were you saying about meeting an interesting lady?"

This time, Lucius interrupted by asking, "Do we have any more of those preserves? They would taste mighty good on these beaten biscuits."

Juno hurried out of the room to bring back more preserves. Again, Tildy could see that Lucius was scowling at her. For some reason he did not want her to tell about Miss Floyd. Maybe he sensed what a fool he had made of himself and didn't want Tildy to let it be known.

Or perhaps he was afraid that Tildy would let slip that after they had talked with Miss Floyd he had grabbed the reins and insisted on driving the wagon.

"Do go on with your story, Tildy," Aunt Rachel said. "What about this woman?"

Tildy couldn't think of any way to get around telling them. She decided to make it as short as possible, however.

"Well, it really didn't amount to much. There was a fine lady in a buggy. She was going in the opposite direction. We visited a bit with her. She invited us to have tea at Rose Hill the next time we were in the vicinity."

Tildy didn't say more, but Lucius was still glaring at her over his soup spoon.

"So, you met the famous Miss Olivia Floyd, did you?" Aunt Rachel said.

"Who in the world is that?" Tildy could tell that Mother's curiosity was piqued.

"She lives on a very grand plantation called Rose Hill. She fancies herself a bit of a fortune-teller, I've heard."

"Yes," Tildy exclaimed, forgetting about her resolve not to tell any more than necessary about the meeting. "She even offered to tell my fortune."

Mother raised her eyebrows. "Oh my goodness. I hope you didn't agree to let her indulge you in that sort of foolishness."

"It's not foolishness," Lucius spoke for the first time. "Miss Floyd knew all about Jubal Early's raid on Washington before it even happened."

"Perhaps she had some advance information," Aunt Rachel suggested. "I understand that she is sometimes in the company of Union as well as Confederate officers."

Tildy noticed that Mother had begun to look more distressed as the story unfolded.

"In fact, the woman appears to enjoy her reputation of being a spy," Aunt Rachel said.

"A spy!" Tildy and her mother exclaimed at almost the same time.

"There is a story that she has managed to send messages through the Union lines to the South," Aunt Rachel said. "The area around Port Tobacco is known to be a hotbed of intrigue, although little comes of it. I have a feeling that the woman thinks it enhances her reputation to have this sort of gossip make the rounds."

"It's not gossip," Lucius defended Miss Floyd. "She is a true supporter of the Southern cause and she has been a great help. I know for a fact . . . ."

Aunt Rachel stared at her son and asked sternly, "And just what is it that you know, Lucius?"

Lucius sat with his mouth gaping open like a fish out of water. He could not seem to find the right words. He did not get a chance to answer, however, for at that moment Uncle Caleb came striding into the room. He threw a folded-up newspaper onto the dining room table.

"Cato found this in the wagon while we were unloading the casks," Uncle Caleb said, pointing at it. "Is this yours, Lucius?"

Lucius looked around frantically as if hoping someone would come to his rescue.

"You and I are going to have a very serious talk, young man," Uncle Caleb said.

Mother stood up quickly from the table and moved toward the doorway. "I shall be in the parlor, Rachel. I have some sewing that I hoped to complete before bedtime." Then Mother turned toward Tildy and said point-edly, "Are you finished with your meal, Tildy?"

Taking her cue from her mother, Tildy also stood and picked up her bowl. "I'll see if Juno has a bit more of this soup." She hurriedly left the room.

Tildy really did not want to know what was going on in the dining room between Lucius and his parents. She couldn't help but hear anyway as Uncle Caleb's angry voice thundered out.

"Where did you get this newspaper, young man?"

"I found it. I found it in Port Tobacco," Lucius said.

Tildy knew that was not the truth. She had seen Lucius take the paper from his own coat pocket to show to the man he had met there.

"Do you know what this is?" Uncle Caleb continued, his voice growing more and more agitated. "It's a Rebel paper."

"Oh no," Aunt Rachel cried out loud enough for Tildy to hear. "Surely it isn't the *Maryland News Sheet*."

"That is exactly what it is," Uncle Caleb stormed. "And, if someone else other than Cato had picked this up in our wagon do you know what would happen?"

If Lucius answered, Tildy could not hear.

"We could be in trouble around here," Uncle Caleb said. "People would think we are Rebels."

This time Tildy could hear Lucius. His volume almost matched that of his father's. "Well, we are Rebels, aren't we? Don't we believe that the Southern cause is right?"

"Yes, we believe in the Southern cause, but not in the things this paper prints. The war is almost over. We are going to get along the best we can, just as we have done all through the war years. The Southern cause is lost."

158

"It's not," Lucius cried. "It's not lost. The war is not over. Things are going to happen. They'll happen soon. I know they will."

"Be still," Uncle Caleb commanded. "I don't want to hear anymore about this from you. I'm going to teach you a lesson to make sure you stay away from people who fill your head with such crazy ideas. Come with me."

"Please Caleb," Aunt Rachel pleaded. "Please. The boy has been ill and he's had a long hard day. Don't punish him. I'm sure he didn't mean to do anything wrong. You can't punish him for simply finding a newspaper."

"I've got to work this foolishness out of him," Uncle Caleb said.

"Lucius," Aunt Rachel begged. "Tell your father that you won't do this sort of thing again. Promise him. Promise me."

All Tildy could hear was the sound of Aunt Rachel sobbing. Then, there was no sound from the dining room.

Tildy sat and looked at the bowl of half-finished soup before her. She no longer felt hungry. What she had heard disturbed her deeply. She could never agree with those who believed in the Southern cause, but somehow she wished that Uncle Caleb had enough courage to stand up for it if he believed in it.

Tildy went quietly to the door and listened. There was no sound from the dining room. Carefully she pushed the door open a bit so that she could see. Lucius, Aunt Rachel, and Uncle Caleb had all gone.

Tildy started to cross the dining room on her way to the hall when she noticed that the offending newspaper had been left lying on the table where Uncle Caleb had put it. She wondered what sort of thing would be in a Rebel newspaper. She paused and glanced at some of the printed articles. One of them caught her full attention immediately.

Bold, black headlines read:

MILLIGAN ARRESTED.

Tildy recalled what Lucius had said to that man in Port Tobacco. The word, "arrested," was one of the few that she could hear of their conversation after Lucius had shown the man the paper. This must have been what they were talking about. Tildy quickly read the short article beneath the headline:

Lambdin P. Milligan, along with certain associates was arrested in Indiana by the military commander of the district. He was accused of conspiracy to release and arm Rebel prisoners. The raid was to have taken place on August 16, 1864. The released prisoners planned to march into the states of Kentucky and Missouri in order to join with other forces to invade Indiana. Milligan will be tried before a military commission.

Tildy could hardly believe what she had just seen. There was more, but before she could continue reading she heard a door slam at the rear of the house, followed by the sound of Uncle Caleb's heavy boots in the back hallway. Tildy dropped the paper back on the table and hurried from the dining room, across the hallway, and into the parlor. Her heart was beating furiously as she sat down opposite her mother on the brocade settee.

160

"Tildy, whatever is the matter? Your face is as white as if you had seen an apparition."

"I'm all right," Tildy said, hoping her voice would not betray her.

"I think perhaps you're tired. You've had a very long, busy day," Mother said. "Let me finish this seam and we'll both go up to bed."

Tildy nodded. "Yes, I think you're right. I would like to go upstairs to bed."

In their little attic room at the top of the narrow steps, Tildy and her mother hardly spoke as they got into their nightclothes. They did not want to awaken Elizabeth and Louisa who were both asleep. Quietly Tildy slipped beneath the covers of her cot. Mother leaned over to kiss her goodnight and then got into her own bed.

As tired as Tildy was, she could not seem to go to sleep. She lay in the darkness thinking about all that had happened that day. Somehow it was as though she were struggling with the pieces of a gigantic puzzle. It wasn't easy to fit everything into its proper place.

The newspaper article had bothered her greatly. She had the feeling, for the first time, that for all his boasting and bragging, perhaps Lucius did know about some secret plan. Lucius had told her that something was going to happen back in August. The more she thought about it, the more she thought that the date printed in the newspaper for the release and arming of the prisoners had been about the right time Lucius had mentioned it. She also remembered that when Lucius was ill he had asked over and over what date it was. He kept wanting to know if it was August 16 yet. At the time she had thought he was merely delirious from his fever. She also remembered how distressed he had seemed that whatever he thought was going to happen had not occurred. According to the newspaper article the leader of that raid had been arrested before it could take place.

Tildy knew that Lucius had told his father a deliberate lie about how he acquired the newspaper. She had been with him the entire day. He had not found the newspaper in Port Tobacco. He had it with him. He had taken it from his inside coat pocket. Tildy wondered where he had gotten the paper. It must have been right here in Surrattsville. But where? The only place she could think of would be Surratt's Tavern. She knew that Lucius sneaked over there every chance he got, even though his parents had expressly forbidden it.

Tildy also wondered where Lucius would have gotten his secret information about the raid planned for August 16. Surely no one would trust him with any important information. Tildy remembered how Miss Floyd had laughed at his pretensions and teased him about being on a secret mission.

Then Tildy thought about that awful man Lucius had talked to in Port Tobacco. He had reminded her of some of the men she had seen coming from Surratt's one day—in fact, the very day that she thought she had seen Lucius hiding beneath the counter at Surratt's. If Lucius had any real secret information he must have gotten it by eavesdropping. She knew for a fact that he was very good at that. Suddenly, she realized that if Lucius had overheard such things at Surratt's, that would mean there were Rebel spies who met there. The very thought of that nearly took her breath away. Was it possible that such things could be going on in an establishment run by such a nice lady as Mrs. Surratt?

Tildy got up out of bed and went over to the window. She looked across the field toward Surratt's place. Even now, when most folks were in bed asleep, there was a light on over there.

Don't be silly, she told herself. That is an inn. Travelers come and go there at all times. Lucius was simply an imaginative young boy with romantic ideas about spies. He isn't well enough to be in the Confederate army himself, so he imagines that he is in on secret things. He is just a self-appointed snoop, Tildy decided.

"Tildy?"

Tildy started as she heard her mother's voice behind her. She had been so deep in her own thoughts that she had not heard her mother get out of bed and come over to the window where she was standing.

"Tildy, are you quite certain that you are feeling all right?"

"Yes, Mother. I just couldn't seem to get to sleep."

"You've had a lot of excitement today from what I gather," Mother said. "Perhaps I shouldn't have let you make that journey to Port Tobacco. I didn't like the sound of some of the things I heard about it."

"No, everything was fine, Mother," Tildy insisted. "I'll go back to bed now. I'm sorry I disturbed you."

"You didn't disturb me, Tildy. I just want to be sure you're not suffering any ill-effects from today. You promise you will tell me if anything is wrong?"

"Yes, Mother," Tildy promised as she turned to go back to her bed. Then, she remembered something else that had happened today.

"Mother," she whispered. "What is a Nu-Oh-Lac?"

"A what?" Mother asked, the surprise evident in her voice.

"A Nu-Oh-Lac," Tildy repeated.

"Wherever did you hear that word, Tildy?"

"I heard it today over in Port Tobacco. Lucius was talking to a man. When he told the man that I was from Indiana, the man asked him if I was a Nu-Oh-Lac."

"And what did you say to that?" Mother wanted to know.

"I didn't say anything. At first, I didn't hear what he said clearly. Then, the more I got to thinking about it, the more I was sure that the word was Nu-Oh-Lac and that I had heard it somewhere before."

"Oh dear, I never should have let you go. It's all my fault," Mother said, sounding very distressed.

"Mother, what is it? What's wrong?" Tildy asked. "You know what the man was talking about, don't you? Tell me what it means."

"It's something I don't even like to think about," Mother said.

Tildy waited, wondering if her mother would say anything else about it. As much as she wanted to know, she sensed that she should not insist that Mother tell.

At last Mother sighed and said, "I suppose I had better tell you. It's a kind of code word."

"A code word? Mother, what is this all about?"

"It's hard to explain," Mother said. "You see, there were some people in the North who were opposed to the

164

war. There were different reasons, but some of them favored the Southern cause. Some of these people had secret societies that they belonged to. One of them was called 'Knights of the Golden Circle.'" Mother paused and Tildy thought perhaps this was all Mother was going to tell her.

"Something happened before your papa went into the army." Another pause. Tildy knew it was very difficult for Mother to talk about whatever it was she had to tell.

"Do you remember that time our old cow wandered off into the woods to have her calf? We thought we'd lost her for good. Your papa was gone for hours looking for her. He liked to never have found her. When he did, he had a terrible time catching her and the calf. They ran him all over the place. It was dark when he finally got them in hand and started home with the two of them."

Mother cleared her throat before continuing. "On the way back, Papa saw that someone had started a fire in the woods. He went over to see about it. When he got closer he saw a bunch of men gathered around a fire. They were having some sort of meeting. He suspected it was the Knights. It was then that the calf bawled and the men spotted your papa. They warned him not to tell anyone what he had seen. You know your papa. He wasn't about to let anybody tell him what to do, especially on his own land. He said he wouldn't promise anything."

For a moment, Tildy thought that was the end of the story, but Mother had more to tell.

"A few nights later we heard noises out in our barn lot. Papa got up and went to see about it. A bunch of men were out there. It looked as though they were trying

165

to set the barn on fire. Papa fired a rifle up in the air and scared them off. As they rode away we could hear them shouting that word."

Mother shivered. She clasped her arms tightly in front of her as though trying to protect herself from the memory. "I'll never forget the way it sounded when they called out 'Nu-Oh-Lac! Nu-Oh-Lac! Nu-Oh-Lac!'"

"But what does it mean?" Tildy asked.

"We found out later. It's the name *Calhoun*, spelled backward. It stands for Calhoun, the secessionist."

"Oh. Mother," Tildy said, reaching out to hug her as the two of them stood close together in the darkness of the attic room. "Why didn't you ever tell me?"

"It would only have made you frightened, especially after Papa was gone away to the army. Sometimes I used to hear noises at night when I was alone with just you three girls. I would be so afraid it was those men coming back."

"What did you do, Mother?"

"I prayed for courage to face whatever had to be faced so that I could take care of all of you,"

"You were very brave, Mother. Papa would have been so proud of you."

Mother didn't speak, but Tildy could feel wet tears on her mother's cheeks.

"Did you ever find out who the men were?"

"They had their faces covered," Mother said. "We thought we recognized some of their voices, but we couldn't be positive."

Later that night after Tildy and Mother had gone back to their own beds, Tildy remembered something. It was almost as if she could hear voices speaking that word.

"Don't let the Nu-Oh-Lac's get you."

She remembered where she had first heard it. It was the day the Pettibone brothers had come over and painted that gray star on the Graham barn. They had been the ones who said it to her the first time. It hadn't meant a thing to her then. Now, she understood.

12

Tildy knew that today was a day that she would never forget. It was Tuesday and it had started much as any other ordinary weekday in the Larrabie household. As usual, Juno had gotten up early and lit the fire in the stove and prepared breakfast for the family. As on every other morning, Cato was out early working with Uncle Caleb and Lucius. And, as they did on every other morning, they came in later to eat their breakfast after having already put in several hours of labor. Linny followed her daily routine of getting the younger Larrabie boys out of bed and dressed and fed. But after that, things changed.

Juno, Linny, and Cato got dressed up in their Sunday "go to-meeting" clothes. Together they walked down the long lane from the Larrabie house to the road. There they became part of a group of other blacks from the Surrattsville neighborhood who were on their way to worship at their little frame church.

The events that led up to this day had been announced on October 29. It was then that the governor of the state of Maryland had issued an official proclamation. He declared that all of Maryland's slaves would be free on the day that the new state constitution went into effect. This was the day . . . Tuesday, November 1, 1864.

Tildy stood on the front verandah of the Larrabie house and watched the people moving along the road. There was some talking and very soft laughter, but mostly Tildy heard singing. Tildy would have given anything to go with Juno and Linny and Cato, but she knew it would be impossible. This was their celebration. Yet, she felt that she had a part in the joy of this day, too. This day had been one of the reasons why Papa had joined the Union army. He wanted all people to be free. He used to tell her that he couldn't be completely free as long as some other people were slaves.

Tildy wanted to get closer to the procession so she followed Juno, Cato, and Linny at a distance, walking down the lane, pausing only when she reached the fence along the road. There she stood, tears in her eyes, trying to be a part of this day. If only Papa could have seen this sight. It would have made him very happy. She couldn't help feeling proud. She wished that somehow she could let these people know that she was glad for them. She wished that they could understand that her family had a part in making this happen through Papa's sacrifice. She wanted them to know that she and her family were not like the Larrabies . . . that the Grahams believed in freedom for all, not just for white folks.

Tildy was tempted to remain out here by the fence watching until they all returned home from church again. It was a chilly day, however, and Tildy had no idea how long she would have to wait. She knew that Juno had wrapped a lunch up in a square of cloth to take with them, so they would probably be gone for hours.

Reluctantly, Tildy turned away from her vantage point at the fence and walked back up the lane to the house. There was always work to do. Perhaps it would be best to get busy. She knew that Mother was trying her best to finish the heavy cloth cloaks she was making for Mrs. Surratt and Anna. Mother had hoped to have them

completed before the Surratts moved to Washington. Although she had put in long hours working on them each day, she had not been able to finish in time. Perhaps she should help Mother with the hemming. Tildy liked to think that with her new determination to succeed she was becoming a passable seamstress.

Now that Linny was gone for the day, Elizabeth, Annabelle, and Roseanne had been pressed into service to watch over the younger children. All was not well in that regard, however, for Tildy could hear Sumter screaming for Linny at the top of his lungs.

Tildy nearly collided with Aunt Rachel who came hurrying along the front hallway. As her aunt passed her, she said, "Tildy, I must see to Summy. I had to leave what I was doing in the kitchen. Could you please get the bread dough into the loaf pans and put them into the oven?"

Tildy went to do as she was told. It seemed that for the rest of the day she was running one errand or another to help fill the void left by Juno or Linny or Cato. In between tasks, Tildy would hurry out to the lane where she could look to see if the procession of freedmen and women was returning from church yet. It was late afternoon when she finally saw them coming along the road. She dashed out to meet them and walk back to the house with them.

To Tildy's disappointment, they did not say much about what had happened that day while they had been gone. Juno was still singing as she went inside. Tildy could hear her getting out the pots and pans to prepare dinner. Linny followed her mother, with Tildy tagging along after the girl.

"How do you feel now that you're free?" Tildy had to know.

"Don't know," Linny said. "Never been free before."

Tildy just had to talk to someone about it. "Cato, it's a great day, isn't it?"

"Reckon it is," was all he said.

"What are you going to do now?"

"I suppose Master Caleb will find something for me to do around the place 'fore it gets all the way dark."

"I don't mean that, Cato," Tildy said in exasperation. "I mean what will you do now that you can go where you want to go and do whatever you want to do."

Cato didn't answer. Tildy couldn't tell what was going on in his mind.

"You know that you don't have to work for my uncle Caleb any more. You can work for whomever you want to and they have to pay you just as they would have to pay any other worker. You and your mother and your sister are free to do whatever you want to do."

"But what are we gonna do?" Cato asked. "We don't know nothing but working for Master Caleb. Where else are we gonna go?"

"Well," Tildy hesitated, then said excitedly, "You can get some land and work it for yourself."

"Buying land costs money," said a voice behind her. It was Lucius. She had not heard him walk up behind her. She hadn't known he was listening to their conversation. Was that why Linny and Cato were being so careful not to say much about how they felt? Didn't they realize that Uncle Caleb didn't have any right to direct their lives anymore?

172

"How are they going to earn enough money to buy land?" Lucius continued.

"Now that you're free, Uncle Caleb will have to pay all of you for the work you do around here," Tildy said to Cato, pointedly ignoring Lucius.

"Oh, Master Caleb already talked to us about that," Cato said. "He's going to give us a place to live and something to eat. That's our pay."

"But that's no different than it was before," Tildy said, outraged at the idea. "That means that nothing has changed."

"That's right," Lucius said, smiling. "That's what I have been trying to tell you."

"The war is almost over," Tildy said. "When the South has surrendered and the Union is restored. . . ."

"The South will never surrender," Lucius stormed at her. "Southerners will never give up."

"Lucius, you just hush up that nonsense." Uncle Caleb had come around the corner of the house and up onto the porch. Tildy wondered just how much of this conversation he had heard. She looked about and noticed that Linny and Cato had left so quickly and quietly, it was almost as though they had disappeared into thin air.

"The South is out of money and out of supplies and out of men. It's time for us to get back to making a living and stop talking about all this foolishness."

"It isn't foolishness," Lucius insisted. "We'll never give up. There are people still doing things. There are plans."

"Lucius," Uncle Caleb said firmly, staring with his cold eyes at his son. "Enough. I don't want to hear any-

173

more about this from you. You don't know what you're talking about."

With that, Caleb Larrabie opened the door and stamped into the house. Tildy heard the back door slam loudly.

Tildy also heard Lucius muttering, half to himself, "Everybody laughs at me. They think I don't know anything, but I do."

He looked up and saw Tildy staring at him. "You're just like everyone else," he said. "You think I'm making this up, but there are plans."

Before Tildy could answer, Lucius continued. "You think I don't know what people say about me? You think I didn't see how Miss Floyd and her driver were laughing? Well, let them make sport of me. Someday people will find out that Miss Floyd is not the only one who can carry messages. There are other ways to help our cause besides wearing a uniform. I'm just as much a part of it as any of them."

Lucius seemed to be growing more agitated by the moment. His face became very red and his eyes glistened feverishly as he talked. Tildy wondered if he were going to become ill again.

"Johnny Surratt is up in Canada now. He's making arrangements for a plan that will let everyone know that the South isn't going to quit . . . ever. There is still plenty of fight left in us."

Tildy stood as though she were hypnotized by Lucius' ravings. At times he did sound as though he really knew something, but common sense told her that this was just wishful thinking on his part. She shook her head in disgust.

174

"Did you read about that raid on the town of St. Albans in Vermont?"

Tildy had not. It wasn't as easy for her to get access to news here in Maryland.

"I thought you prided yourself on being so well informed," Lucius said, gleefully. "It appears to me that whenever anything comes along that has to do with a Southern victory, you close your eyes to it."

Tildy did not know what to answer, but it didn't matter. Lucius was bursting to enlighten her.

"Well, on October 19, a party of secessionists crossed the Canadian border and took possession of the village of St. Albans. They managed to escape with $200,000 from the banks there."

"So, what does that prove except that they were a bunch of thieves?" Tildy said.

"What do you think that kind of money could be used for?" Lucius asked.

"I suppose it could be used to buy guns or something." Tildy wished that she had not let Lucius draw her into this conversation in the first place. Hoping to end it, she said, "But, the South hasn't got enough men left to fight, so they certainly don't need money to buy guns."

She started to walk away when Lucius said, "If the Southern prisoners of war were freed, that might make a difference, wouldn't it?"

By now Tildy was growing exasperated with Lucius' crazy ideas. "And, just how is the South going to free the prisoners held by the Union?"

Lucius suddenly lowered his voice. "What do you suppose would happen if Old Abe himself were captured? What if he were taken prisoner of war?" Lucius

175

stopped abruptly as though he had been goaded into saying more than he had intended. Lucius took a step closer to Tildy and said in a tone that sounded threatening to Tildy. "You just wait and see. . . . But when something happens, you had better never tell anyone what I told you, or else. . . . "

"Or else what?" Tildy asked. "Just what will you do?"

"I'll tell my mother and your mother that you disobeyed them when we went to Port Tobacco."

"What do you mean?" Tildy wanted to know what wild thing he could possibly have invented.

"I'll tell them how you let me drive the wagon."

"Lucius Larrabie!" Tildy almost choked with anger at him. "You are the one who grabbed the reins out of my hands and insisted on driving the wagon."

"Do you think my mother would believe that?"

Tildy was so flabbergasted she could not think of an answer. Instead, she lashed out with, "I think you are crazy, Lucius. You are completely crazy."

"Just wait and see," Lucius said. "Just you wait and see."

Tildy turned her back on her cousin and went inside the house. How could she have even imagined for a minute that Lucius might actually have known something? She was beginning to think that he really was crazy. Maybe the long fever had affected his brain.

The day had been ruined for Tildy. It had started out to be something so special, but Lucius and Uncle Caleb had managed to ruin it for her. Even Juno and Linny and Cato had spoiled her happiness. They had not been as joyful and excited as she had expected them to be. She had half-imagined them running and jumping and shouting because of what had happened. She had expected to see them pack up their belongings and move away to a wonderful, new, free life. Instead, they had come back from church to the Larrabie house just as though it were any other day. Juno went on cooking dinner. Linny kept on taking care of Sumter and Edmund and Jefferson and Calhoun. Cato was probably out in back stacking wood before it got dark.

Didn't they know . . . didn't they care that hundreds, yes, thousands of men had died so that they wouldn't have to be slaves anymore?

And Caleb Larrabie was the worst of all. He hadn't given up a thing. Even though the state of Maryland had proclaimed that slavery was over, Uncle Caleb was still making slaves of Juno and Linny and Cato. He gave them only what he had given them before and now he called it wages.

Caleb Larrabie didn't care about the South's cause. Slave or free didn't mean anything to him. He just wanted life to go on here as it always had. He just wanted to get on with making a living. He wanted to keep on pretending that he was rich and that he was a fine gentleman. He didn't care one way or another who won the war.

In a way, Tildy thought bitterly, the South had won. It was she and Mother and Elizabeth and Louisa who had lost. They had lost Papa. They had lost the farm. Their lives had changed completely.

Tildy's eyes were burning with tears as she quickly climbed the stairs to the third floor attic room that she shared with her mother and sisters. It was dark and

177

gloomy up there. It matched her mood perfectly. She threw herself down on her narrow cot and cried. Tildy pressed her face into the pillow and cried loud, long sobs.

"Tildy, whatever is the matter with you?" It was Mother standing over her. "What has happened? Are you all right?"

Tildy couldn't speak. Mother kneeled down beside the little bed and put her arms about Tildy. She rocked back and forth gently cradling Tildy, until her tears had subsided.

"Oh, Mother," Tildy said. "Why can't things be the way they were? I hate it here. I hate Lucius and Uncle Caleb."

Mother continued to hold her.

"It just isn't fair," Tildy said.

"No, it isn't fair," Mother said. "Life isn't always fair. Sometimes it's very bitter, but I am not going to let that make me a bitter person. Bitter people are not at all pleasant to be around."

"You mean like Uncle Caleb?"

Mother didn't answer.

"We can't always help what happens to us from the outside, but we can decide how we are going to be on the inside."

Tildy knew that whatever happened she didn't want to get to be like Uncle Caleb.

Tildy pressed her head against Mother's shoulder. It was good to have Mother's comforting arms about her. No, whatever happened, she wasn't going to let herself become like Uncle Caleb.

178

13

It seemed to Tildy that she had never spent a drearier winter than the one she spent in Maryland. She hated being cooped up in the house all day long. She missed her school back in Indiana. The Larrabie children did not go to a regular school. Uncle Caleb said that there was no money to spend this year to pay for his own children to attend the subscription school. So, of course that meant that there was no way for Tildy or Elizabeth to go either.

It did little to ease Tildy's great disappointment that each day the dining room was turned into a classroom for a couple of hours with Aunt Rachel and Mother or sometimes, even Tildy herself, acting as a teacher for the younger children.

Tildy had to admit that she did enjoy taking her turns teaching, especially when it came to history lessons. It had always been her favorite subject and she tried to make it especially interesting because Linny was often in the dining room, too, to help keep the boys in order. Tildy would sometimes act out certain events, dressing up in makeshift costumes that she had collected from the rag bag that Juno kept under the back stairs. Sometimes she had a hard time staying in character when she acted out George Washington crossing the Delaware or Thomas Jefferson writing the Declaration of Independence, because she kept stealing glances at Linny to see if the young woman showed signs that she understood what it was all about. Tildy thought that it was just too bad that Cato couldn't be present, too. She felt more than repaid for her efforts when she heard Linny describing the day's lessons to Cato one evening.

In spite of the dining room school dramatics, most of the time the gloomy months passed slowly for Tildy. The worst thing was that there seemed to be nothing for her to look forward to.

There was one bright spot when Mother said that she had to make a trip to Washington City. Mrs. Surratt had ordered more dresses for herself and Anna. Mother had the material cut and basted together and needed to do the fitting of them before she put in the permanent stitches. Aunt Rachel was feeling a bit poorly again and Tildy was allowed to go along in her place.

Surprisingly, the day turned out to be quite enjoyable even though Lucius also went along to drive the buggy. Uncle Caleb had insisted that it wasn't proper for two lone females to be driving about the city unescorted by a man. Wisely, Tildy made no comments about considering her gawky young cousin a man. She wanted to do or say nothing that would cast a shadow over the excitement of such an outing. Tildy decided that Lucius was so happy to be allowed to skip his farm chores for a day and go along as driver that he appeared to be trying very hard to be charming.

Perhaps they were all determined to make this a special occasion, for they each chatted companionably as Lucius helped both Tildy and Mother into the buggy. He was careful to make certain that the lap robe was tucked in about their feet to prevent any drafts from making them uncomfortable as they rode along.

As with all of the possessions that Uncle Caleb showed to the world, his buggy was a neat little rig. Cato had been ordered out early that morning to make sure that it was polished up before they started out.

"Are you quite comfortable?" Lucius inquired once they were settled. Tildy could only stare in amazement at such politeness from her cousin, but Mother answered matter-of-factly as though such courtesy were the rule instead of the exception, "Yes, thank you. I'm sure we are going to make a very pleasant day of it." Mother turned out to be right. It was one of those spring-like days that comes along during the grayest of seasons. Tildy sometimes thought they were sent so that people could manage to endure the rest of the winter. Tildy sucked the clean, mild air deep into her lungs as though to wash away all the stale, mustiness of the past few months. She even enjoyed hearing Lucius whistling merrily. If this were a dream, she planned to let it last as long as possible.

"Just look at those crocuses," Mother sighed happily as the buggy rattled over the rutted road. "And listen to the birds. They sound as happy as we are for this day."

Everything was going well until they approached the long wooden Navy Yard Bridge over the Potomac River that led to the city. Lucius pulled up on the reins and the horse stopped by the guard station.

When the soldier on duty asked why they wanted to cross the bridge, Lucius replied, "We are going into Washington on business."

Tildy heard a soldier who was standing nearby say, "And, just what business would Johnny Rebs have in Washington?"

Another soldier laughed at this unofficial query.

Tildy's face burned. How dare they refer to her and Mother as Rebs? She started to tell them in no uncertain terms that her papa had volunteered for the Union army. He had been in battle, not stationed safely assigned to guarding a bridge where they could insult people as these men were. Before she could set them straight, she felt Mother's hand firmly on hers. At that pressure she glanced at her mother and saw Mother shake her head ever so slightly. Tildy understood that she was being warned to keep silent and managed to do so, but it was with a great deal of effort.

Tildy was more than a little surprised when Lucius responded with a sickly sweet smile and the startling words, "We've got an appointment with the President. We have a favor to ask."

On hearing that, the guards laughed loudly and one of them came forward and slapped his hand loudly on the horse's flank. "Well, you'd best hurry. You'll have to wait in line. Everyone else in the country is at the President's house lined up to ask a favor."

The soldier's hand smacking the horse caused the animal to lurch forward and Tildy and her mother were thrown forward and backward with a sudden jolting.

Tildy could hear the soldiers still laughing as the buggy bumped onto the wooden bridge. Lucius was laughing, too.

When Mother had regained her composure she said, "Lucius, whatever made you say a thing like that?"

Tildy could tell that Mother was upset by the incident and Lucius must have realized that he had gone too far.

"Please forgive me, Aunt Rebecca. I meant it as a bit of a joke, but I see that it was in bad taste. I hope you won't let that bit of unpleasantness spoil the day."

"Of course, Lucius. We shall pretend that it never happened," Mother said quietly.

Lucius seemed eager to make amends as well as to demonstrate his knowledge of the city. He gave them a brief tour of points of interest on their way to Mrs. Surratt's boardinghouse.

"I have to be careful which streets we take. Brownie doesn't like the street cars, do you, Brownie girl?"

The horse arched her neck prettily and snorted as though she knew what Lucius had said.

"There now, straight ahead of us," Lucius pointed out. "There is the monument that was being built to honor George Washington."

Tildy saw a tall, but unfinished white obelisk on a rise of ground near the Potomac. Around its base was a rag-tag collection of small wooden shacks.

"Inside those sheds are stored the blocks to finish it. Someday it will be a grand structure."

"My goodness," Mother said. "It stands quite tall now. I've never in my life seen a structure that high. How much farther up do they intend to go with it?"

"When the capstone is in place," Lucius said knowledgeably, "It will be at least three times the height it is now."

Tildy and her mother stared at the monument, marveling at it while Lucius sat proudly as though he had something to do with it.

The next stop was in front of the Capitol Building. They could hear the sound of hammers from the huge dome that topped the sprawling building.

"Work never stopped on the dome throughout the hostilities," Lucius said. "The statue was put in place atop the dome almost two years ago, but there is still finishing-up work to be done on it."

Lucius continued to point out various attractions until at last the buggy had traveled to the 500 block of "H" Street and stopped in front of a three story, gray brick house. It seemed quite a fine place to Tildy. It had a front porch edged with iron grillwork. A small patch of green lay between the house and the corner. It did not appear much different from the other houses on the street.

Lucius, still seeming to be on his very best behavior, jumped from his perch on the driver's seat and hurried around to help both Tildy and Mother get down from the buggy. He then positioned himself between the two of them. He put one hand under Mother's elbow and another under Tildy's and escorted both of them to the front door.

Anna Surratt opened the door and welcomed them as though her visitors had been long-lost relatives rather than acquaintances of only a few months. Such laughter and chattering and scurrying about made the entire scene seem more like a party than a routine dress fitting.

"How are Elizabeth and little Louisa?" Mrs. Surratt wanted to know. "And, tell me all about Rachel and her children. How lucky she is to have you there to help her. How she managed before you came I shall never know."

Mother and Tildy told everything they could think of that Anna and Mrs. Surratt might be the least bit interested in.

"Now, tell me how you find your life in the capital city?" Mother asked.

"I'm usually quite busily occupied with the boarding-house," Mrs. Surratt said. "One of the nicest things is that some of my guests are family and others are old friends. Most are permanent, although there are some who come and go . . . mostly friends of Johnny's."

This casual exchange at last blended into talk about the real purpose of Mother's visit. Mother fitted Anna first for the two dresses she was making for her. After that was done and Mrs. Surratt was being fitted, Anna and Tildy continued their visit in the parlor.

"I notice that you still have your favorite picture," Tildy said, nodding in the direction of the framed portrayal on the mantle.

Tildy was certain that she noticed a rosy glow color up Anna's cheeks at the mention of it.

Tildy was surprised when Anna reached for the picture and handed it to Tildy.

"It's a very special picture," Anna said.

Try as she might, Tildy could not really see anything out of the ordinary about it. Tildy supposed that the reason for the coy manner in which Anna behaved when she talked about it was that it must be special for some other reason than its artistic value.

"I'll bet it was a gift to you," Tildy said.

"As a matter of fact, it was," Anna said. "How did you know that?"

"You seem to treasure it so," Tildy said. "And, I recall the way you gazed at it when you played those sad songs at the piano on the first day I met you back in Surrattsville."

Anna laughed. "You are clever, but what I like best about it is on the back and not on the front."

Tildy turned the picture over. On the back was another picture. This one was the likeness of a very handsome young man. A man with dark hair and the most expressive eyes Tildy had ever seen. Even though it was just a picture, Tildy could almost feel those dark eyes glaring at her. He had such an intense expression, it almost made Tildy uncomfortable to look at it. For some reason that she could not explain, she had a feeling that she would not like this person if she were to meet him. She wondered why Anna would have this man's likeness in back of the picture. Then the reason occurred to her.

"Is this your gentleman friend?" Tildy blurted out.

Again Anna's cheeks flamed.

"Oh, I am so sorry," Tildy apologized quickly. "I didn't mean to speak out of turn. It was rude of me."

Anna giggled and said, "It's all right. No, he is not my gentleman friend, though I wish . . . ." Anna didn't complete her sentence and the idea hung in the air between them.

"I must say he is quite handsome," Tildy admitted. "Does he live here at the boardinghouse?"

"Actually, he lives in Maryland but he travels about a good deal so that he seems to live many places." Anna paused and looked at Tildy with a strange puzzled expression. "Do you actually mean to tell me that you do not recognize him?"

Tildy stared at the picture again. There was something vaguely familiar about the man, but she could not recall where she might have seen him.

"Perhaps," Tildy suggested, "Perhaps I saw him at the tavern when you lived in Surrattsville. Was he ever a guest there?"

Anna blushed again. "Yes, he has visited our tavern there and he comes to see us here at the boardinghouse, too."

"Oh, then surely I must have seen him when he was in the Surrattsville neighborhood."

Anna shook her head in a way that indicated that she was amazed at what Tildy had just said. "Matilda Graham, do you mean to tell me that you really do not know who the person in this picture is?"

Tildy could only shake her head.

"This is John Wilkes Booth!" Anna said.

Tildy stood without registering any expression. Anna repeated the name, with emphasis on each syllable of the name she had spoken before. "I said that this is a picture of John Wilkes Booth. Booth, the famous stage actor."

Now it was Tildy's turn to blush. She was embarrassed at having to admit that she was ignorant of a person whom Anna seemed to be so impressed with. "I'm so sorry, but I have never heard that name before."

"Then you must be the only person in the entire world who has not," Anna said, with more than a bit of exasperation evident in her tone of voice.

Tildy hoped she had not offended her friend. "I'm sure he must be a very great man, but you see, we lived a long way out in the country in Indiana. We did not have a chance there to see such things as stage plays. I don't know the names of any actors. I'm sure he is very famous and just because I have never heard of him does not take away from his importance at all."

Suddenly, Anna glanced toward the parlor doorway. "Someone's coming," she whispered and she moved hurriedly to replace the picture back on the mantle just as it had been before with Mr. Booth's likeness turned to the wall. "Please don't say a word about your having seen that picture on the back. My brother was very angry when he learned that I had purchased this likeness. He told me throw it away, but I just couldn't. So, I hid it there on the back of the picture called 'Morning, Noon, and Night.' That way I can see it when I wish and my brother Johnny doesn't have to know."

Tildy didn't understand. "Doesn't your brother like Mr. Booth?"

"Oh, they are friends," Anna said.

"Then why doesn't your brother want you to . . . ?" Tildy did not have a chance to complete her sentence for at that moment Mrs. Surratt and Mother came back into the room.

Anna put her fingers up to her lips and nodded her head in the direction of the picture sitting so innocently on the mantle.

Tildy put her own fingers to her lips as a sign that she understood and would say nothing.

"Have you two young ladies been having a nice visit?" Mrs. Surratt asked.

"Oh yes, ma'am," Tildy answered politely as Anna giggled.

"Then I think it is time for us to have our little tea party," Mrs. Surratt suggested.

"Please, don't go to any trouble for us," Mother said.

"I assure you that it is no trouble at all. In fact, we have been looking forward to having you visit."

Tildy liked the way Mrs. Surratt made her and her mother feel as though they were valued friends instead of just someone she paid to do sewing for her.

The tea and cakes that Mrs. Surratt served were delicious as usual and served so nicely in pretty little china plates and cups that Tildy felt quite grand. She wished that the day would never have to end. She was disappointed when a clock on the mantle chimed, calling attention to the hour.

"Oh, dear me," Mother said. "I had no idea it was so late. Where does the time go?"

"It evaporates when company is so pleasant," Mrs. Surratt said, sounding as though she were as disappointed as they that the visit must end.

"You must be sure and stop in to see us when your business brings you back to Surrattsville," Mother invited.

"I should love to, but perhaps it would be best if you and Rachel came to the tavern to see me there. You must know that Caleb Larrabie and I . . . well, we tend to rub each other's fur the wrong way."

As they stood and started to leave the parlor, Mother looked about and said, "Why, where in the world is Lucius?"

Tildy realized that they had not seen anything of him since they had arrived. That had been almost three hours ago. She had been having such a good time that she had not even missed him.

"I'm surprised that he didn't appear when we had the tea and cakes," Tildy said.

"He was probably upstairs with Johnny," Anna said. "You know how Lucius always manages to be wherever Johnny is. He has been Johnny's shadow for years."

"Yes, that's probably where he is. Anna, would you go upstairs and tell him that Mrs. Graham is ready to leave now?" Mrs. Surratt turned to Mother, "Johnny is home for a few days. His business takes him away a good deal of the time."

"Just what kind of work has your Johnny found to do?" Mother asked.

It seemed to Tildy that Mrs. Surratt suddenly seemed quite flustered. "Well he did have a job here in town . . . but that didn't work out for him. Johnny just can't seem to stand being cooped up in an office all day. So now he . . . well, he travels around a good bit." Mrs. Surratt laughed a strange little laugh and shrugged her shoulders. "He says that women shouldn't bother their heads about men's business. I suppose he thinks I wouldn't be able to understand what he was doing."

Tildy couldn't help but think that was a bit odd. How could Mrs. Surratt's son underestimate his mother's ability that way? Aunt Rachel had often said that Mary Surratt did a better job of running the tavern business than her husband had when he had been alive. In fact, Aunt Rachel declared that if it hadn't been for Mary Surratt the business would have gone right down the drain and that the burden of it had rested on her most of the time. Tildy supposed that Johnny Surratt must be another of those men like Uncle Caleb who think women have to be treated like hothouse plants.

When Anna returned with Lucius in tow, Mrs. Surratt said, "The tea is quite cold by now but do take as many of those little cakes as you can eat on the way home."

"We really must go now," Mother insisted as Lucius selected several dainty goodies to stuff in his pockets. "It has been such a lovely afternoon. Thank you."

"It was truly our pleasure," Mrs. Surratt said. "Do come again."

"Yes, do come again," Anna echoed and looked right at Tildy and then glanced over at the picture on the mantle. She smiled what seemed to Tildy to be a conspiratorial smile. Tildy smiled back the same way. It was fun to think that they shared a secret about the picture behind a picture.

As the buggy rolled over the cobbled streets of Washington none of them spoke. Each of them seemed engrossed in his or her own special review of the day. It wasn't until they approached the Navy Yard Bridge that the silence was broken.

"It has been a lovely day, hasn't it?" Mother asked.

Lucius and Tildy both agreed wholeheartedly.

"I hope that it will continue to be a lovely day with nothing said or done to spoil it," Mother said.

191

Tildy was certain that was a distinct warning to Lucius and he must have taken it as such for he was on his very best behavior as they passed the guard this time.

"This has been the kind of day," Tildy said happily, as the Larrabie place finally came into view, "that you save up for remembering in the deep of winter. I think I'll remember this day for a long time to come."

"I know that I'll remember today forever," Lucius said.

Tildy felt a peculiar little tingle slither down her spine as Lucius spoke. She had a feeling that Lucius' words carried a far different meaning than she had meant by her own. She pulled her shawl closer about her shoulders. She suddenly felt chilly. Was it just because the sun was going down or was it something else?

14

Mother was crying! A hot lump of fear burned deep in Tildy's stomach when she heard the awful sound coming from inside the parlor. Tildy shoved the door to that room open and rushed inside. It was mid-day but the draperies were tightly drawn. In the gloom Tildy saw her mother and Aunt Rachel standing with their arms about each other.

"Mother, what's wrong?" Tildy cried out. "Are you ill?"

Mother tried to say something, but her words were muzzy because of her sobbing.

Aunt Rachel turned to Tildy and said, "It's over, Tildy. The Confederate capital has fallen."

Tildy couldn't seem to make sense of what Aunt Rachel was telling her.

"General Lee has surrendered," Aunt Rachel said.

Tildy wondered what that all had to do with Mother's weeping. "What's wrong with my mother?"

"The war is over," Aunt Rachel said.

It was then that Mother was able to speak so that Tildy could understand her painfully drawn out sentence, "Yes, it's over . . . but Jeremiah won't be coming home to us again . . . not ever. . . ."

Tildy saw Mother sag limply against Aunt Rachel.

Tildy didn't know what to do. It frightened her to see Mother crying like that. Tildy felt helpless. Quietly she backed out of the parlor wanting to find a secluded corner where she could be alone with the terrible understanding that was beginning to suffocate her. Suddenly she had to have fresh air to breathe. She stumbled through the hallway to the rear door of the house. She went outside and onto the back verandah where she huddled in one corner.

"The war is over," she whispered to herself. "It's really over."

It still did not seem real. She might have believed it if there had been a celebration. But there were no bells ringing and no bands playing. There was no one laughing and singing and dancing for joy. Instead there were two women standing in a darkened parlor. There were stinging, bitter tears. There was the miserable knowledge that even though the war was over and the fighting had stopped, Papa would not return. The end of the war had not changed that at all. Maybe the fact that he was dead was more real to her now than it had been when the first news had come to them not quite a year ago. He had been away for so long and his absence had been hard to bear, but they had received letters from him. They had lived with the hope that when the war was over he would be back. *How many times each day had they started a sentence with the words, "When the war is over and Papa comes home again. . . ?"* Now, the war was over and that long ago hope that everything would be all right once Papa came home was just an empty hope. Other men would be coming home, but not Papa.

Tildy was so overwhelmed by her own sorrow that she did not hear the back door open. Neither did she hear the soft steps on the porch behind her. It was not until she felt Mother's arm around her shoulder that Tildy realized that she was not alone.

Mother sat down beside her. Tildy leaned toward her mother and put her head in Mother's lap. Mother's gentle fingers soothed Tildy's forehead. Neither of them spoke. They sat like this for what seemed a long time.

At last Mother said, "Let's go for a walk, Tildy. Let's walk and take in the clean fresh air. It will make us feel better."

"Will we ever feel better again, Mother?"

"Sometimes it doesn't seem as though we will," and Tildy was glad that Mother was honest and didn't try to say things just to make her feel good.

They walked together, arm in arm. Slowly, they went down the long lane leading from the Larrabie house. When they reached the fence that ran along the front of the property, they turned and walked along New Cut Road, letting the spring green heal them.

Up ahead Tildy saw a woman dressed in black getting out of a buggy in front of the tavern.

"Look, Mother. Isn't that Mrs. Surratt?"

"It appears to be," Mother said.

"Let's go and say 'hello' to her," Tildy suggested. "Perhaps Anna came along with her."

When they got closer Tildy was disappointed to see that Anna was not in the buggy. Mrs. Surratt, herself, was so distracted by errands that she didn't really have time to visit. She was polite, as usual, explaining, "I've come all the way out here to get some important matters cleared up. I hope you will excuse me for not being able to invite you inside for a nice chat. If I can just get this bothersome matter attended to, perhaps we will be able to move back to Maryland. Then we shall have time to be neighborly."

Tildy was more than surprised to hear Mrs. Surratt say that she hoped to move back to Surrattsville. It had been only a few months ago that she had appeared so anxious to get her son Johnny away from this place. Tildy wondered what had happened to change her mind so soon.

By the time Tildy and Mother had returned to the Larrabie's after their walk, Tildy was feeling much better. For the first time in many months, Tildy again had something to look forward to. After they had talked briefly with Mrs. Surratt and Tildy had thought about Mrs. Surratt moving back to the tavern, Tildy herself had an idea about moving. She broached it very carefully.

"Mother, you seem to be kept very busy with your sewing these days."

"Indeed, I am. I can hardly keep up with all the work I have been asked to do by the ladies in Surrattsville."

"Does that mean you are earning quite a bit of money?"

Mother smiled. "Well, I wouldn't exactly say that we are going to become wealthy on what I am able to earn, but I must admit that I am doing better than I had expected to do."

"I didn't expect that we would be rich," Tildy said, trying to choose her words carefully. "But, do you suppose that we will ever be able to earn enough money to pay our own way?"

"We are paying our own way here, Tildy."

Tildy thought that she detected a note of pride in Mother's voice. "I pay for every bit of food that you and I and your little sisters eat. I also pay something for the roof that we have over our heads. We aren't exactly charity cases."

"In spite of what Lucius says," Tildy murmured.

"What did you say?" Mother asked.

"Nothing," Tildy said quickly, not wanting to let her idea become lost in a discussion of Lucius' unfair taunts.

"Do you suppose . . . " Tildy asked hesitantly, "that you earn enough money for us to be able to live in a house of our very own?" Quickly she added, "A very small house. It would only have to be large enough for the four of us."

"I don't know about that," Mother said. "There are other expenses to consider besides the rent and food when one lives in a house. There would be firewood and lamp oil and . . . ."

"Could we put all the expenses down on paper and then see how much sewing it would take to earn enough to live by ourselves?"

"Yes, we can do that, but I must tell you Tildy that I'm taking in just about all the orders I can possibly fulfill right now. So, I don't want you to be disappointed if we can't afford to do what you want to do."

"What if I helped you more?" Tildy suggested. "I am trying to be much more careful with my sewing. I think my stitches are improving somewhat, aren't they?"

Mother laughed and squeezed Tildy's hand. "Yes, dear, I think you are doing ever so much better."

"It's like Papa told me. I can do anything I really put my mind to. If it meant that we could get a little house of our own and didn't have to be dependent upon Uncle Caleb, I couldn't help but improve."

"I must admit, I wouldn't mind being on our own," Mother said.

With that bit of encouragement, Tildy's fertile mind grew a crop of possibilities. "Elizabeth could help, too. In fact, I think that she is a much better seamstress than I am even though she is younger, and since she enjoys it so much she would be of real assistance doing something other than embroidering useless pieces."

"I have to admit that your sister's stitchery is very promising."

"And, we need to get her away from here where Annabelle and Roseanne constantly fill her head full of silly ideas about being a grand lady. She's getting quite spoiled."

Mother took a very deep breath. "The only thing I can promise you right now is that I will think about it and see if anything can be done."

"Oh, I love you so much," Tildy said and hugged her mother tightly. "Thank you. It is going to be so wonderful to be a close family again in a little house all our very own."

"Remember," Mother cautioned. "I only promised to give it some thought. I don't want you to get your heart set on something and then have to be disappointed."

"I know," Tildy said. "It's only a dream right now, but I shall work very hard and help you in every way that I can."

Mother squeezed her hand again.

Tildy was so full of excitement that she couldn't help but run on about the possibilities. "Maybe we could ask about the neighborhood and see if there isn't a little house somewhere that would be right for us and we could write to Reverend Martin and have him send Papa's desk to us and we could plant a little garden and maybe we could get a cow and . . . . "

"Oh, Tildy, Tildy," Mother said, laughing and shaking her head. "The very things I love most about you are the things that sometimes make me the most fearful for you."

"But Mother, don't you remember that Papa always told us how he came to this country with nothing but hope in his pocket?" Tildy reminded. "It's all right for me to hope, isn't it?"

"Yes, Tildy dear, it's just fine to be hopeful but I don't want you to get hurt by hoping for more than you can really do. I fear sometimes for your eagerness, your impulsiveness. Sometimes you do tend to tackle more than is realistic."

Mother paused and a faraway look came into her eyes as though she were remembering something that was both happy and sad all at once. "Perhaps I shouldn't throw cold water on your enthusiasm. That part of you is so much like Papa. Sometimes I am too cautious. Papa thought I was."

"Maybe that is why the two of you were so happy together. Papa was the dreamer and you were the careful one and you balanced each other."

Mother turned and looked at Tildy for a long time. "Out of the mouths of babes," she said.

Tildy wondered whatever in the world Mother could have meant by that!

The next few days seemed to pass very quickly for Tildy. Perhaps it was because she managed to keep so busy. Now that she had a dream, she couldn't work hard enough to make it come true. She was usually the first one down for breakfast each morning. She would gulp her food and hurry to the parlor where she would be hard at work when Mother came in. Never before in her life had she managed to sit in a chair without fidgeting for so many long hours as she did now. It was all Mother could do to get her to stop for meals or even to quit in the evening when the light was so dim.

"Tildy, you are going to ruin your eyes," Aunt Rachel fretted. "Now, this is Good Friday. You put down your sewing and come along to church with your mother and me and the girls."

Tildy could hardly bear to put down the bright yellow lawn skirt that she was basting.

"Yes, come along Tildy. This is a day of prayer and thanksgiving. The President has decreed it as such," Mother said. "I think it would do us both a world of good to get away from the sewing for a while. We'll work much better when we have refreshed our spirits."

Although the day had started out rather dreary, by the time they came back to the Larrabie place after church, the sun had come out. The weather was quite pleasant, although a bit on the cool side. Tildy held the door open as the others went inside the house.

Tildy lingered for a moment enjoying the fresh air. If she hadn't felt the need to get as much sewing done as possible each day, Tildy would have preferred to stay outside. She looked longingly toward the fields and the greening woods beyond. She wondered if it would be possible to find the meaty kind of mushrooms here in Maryland that she and Papa had hunted for at home in Indiana.

She sighed. Perhaps when the weather warmed up a bit more she would be able to work at her sewing out on the verandah.

She turned to go inside the house and back to work when she happened to see Lucius. He was coming from the field that lay between Larrabie's and the Surratt place. Tildy wondered what it could be that fascinated him so much about the tavern. He continually risked getting into trouble with his father by going over there even after he had been told not to do so.

She realized that Lucius had seen her watching him. He altered his course slightly and headed in her direction. Tildy went inside the house quickly. She did not have anything to say to him.

Lucius managed to catch up with her as she was taking off her bonnet in the front hallway.

"You saw where I have been, didn't you?" he whispered. "You had better not tell anyone."

She refused to lower her voice, "Lucius, I don't care a bit where you have been. I have more important things to do than to play your childish games."

She started to open the parlor door, but he grabbed her arm angrily and pulled her across the hall and into the dining room.

"You'll not be acting so high and mighty after tomorrow," he said.

"And just what does that mean?" Tildy wanted to know.

"It means that everything will have changed by tomorrow. The South will show everyone who has the bravest soldiers after all."

"Lucius, I cannot believe that you are still talking that way. The war is over. Even General Lee has accepted that fact. Why can't you?"

"The war may be over for some, but not for everyone. There are those who will never, ever as long as they live give up the cause of the South."

"Do you mean to tell me that there are still a few people foolish enough to think that anything can be accomplished by trying to continue the rebellion?"

Lucius said, "That is right. And there are more than just a few."

"Lucius Larrabie," Tildy said in exasperation. "Ever since I have been here in Maryland, you have been telling me about secret plans. As far as I can see, nothing has ever come of it, and I don't believe anything ever will."

"It wasn't for lack of trying," Lucius said. "And, they'll keep on trying until the South is vindicated."

Tildy shook her head in disbelief that he could cling to such farfetched notions and not see how silly he sounded. "If all these wonderful plans failed so many times before, what makes you think they are possibly going to succeed now?"

"Because . . . because . . ." Lucius almost choked in his frustration.

"The truth is that you made all of this up. It's wishful

202

thinking. You don't know a thing about any plans because there are no plans. You're imagining things. And if you keep on this way everybody else is going to find out you're as daft as I think you are."

Tildy turned and started to flounce out of the room, but Lucius grabbed at her arm again, bruising it.

"I'm not crazy and I'm not making anything up. I was just over at Surratt's and I saw Mrs. Surratt leave a package for John Lloyd, the man who runs the tavern for her now."

"What kind of a package?" Tildy wanted to know.

"Things that can be used to carry out a secret mission," Lucius said. "Spyglasses. Things like that."

"Just how do you know what was in the package?" Tildy asked.

"I saw John Lloyd unwrap it after Mrs. Surratt left so that he could look and see what was in it," Lucius said, seeming eager to convince her of the truth of what he had to say. "And, I know of other packages that have been brought to the tavern. I've seen where guns are hidden upstairs."

Tildy was outraged that Lucius would think she would believe such a thing. "Are you trying to tell me that a woman such as Mary Surratt is involved in some kind of a Rebel plot . . . that she's a spy?"

"No," Lucius said. "I don't think Mrs. Surratt knows what is going on."

"Well, then why would she deliver that package?"

"She probably did it because Johnny or Mr. Booth or one of the others asked her to do it."

"Are you trying to tell me that Johnny Surratt and that actor are in on some sort of a secret plot?"

"Yes. Not only them, but that man you saw me talking to that day in Port Tobacco. There are others, too."

"How do you know all this?" Tildy demanded.

"I know these people. They come and go at the tavern and I saw two of them at the boardinghouse the day we visited the Surratt's in Washington."

"And, are you going to take part in this mission?"

Lucius hesitated. "Not exactly."

"What does that mean?"

Lucius looked everywhere but never directly at Tildy. "It means that I have heard them talking. And, once I carried a message."

Tildy didn't know what to make of all this, but before she could say anything Lucius said, "I also heard what Mrs. Surratt told Mr. Lloyd when she gave him the package this afternoon."

"And just what did you hear her say?" Tildy asked.

"Mrs. Surratt said, 'These things will be called for tonight!' That means that the plan is going to happen sometime later today."

"And what is the plan, Lucius?"

Again Lucius' eyes shifted uncomfortably from his feet to the ceiling above.

"I don't know exactly," he admitted. "Except that it has something to do with President Lincoln."

"You're out of your mind, Lucius," Tildy said. "I don't believe a word you are saying."

"It's true," Lucius said and for the first time he looked squarely at Tildy. "It's true."

Lucius let go of her arm and left her standing alone in the dining room.

15

Tildy stood alone in the dining room after Lucius had stalked out. She could feel the painful impressions on her arm where he had dug his thin fingers into the flesh. She felt short of breath and her heart was thudding inside her chest.

What was wrong with that boy? In her anger she had called him crazy. Certainly anyone who would make up a terrible thing such as he had told her had to be unbalanced. If he was irrational somebody ought to be told about it. He shouldn't be allowed to be running about saying such awful things. Despite his warning, Tildy thought she ought to speak to his parents about it, but she was not about to go to Uncle Caleb with such a tale. And, how could she tell a dear person such as Aunt Rachel that her oldest son was out of his mind? Tildy didn't know how she could do it.

The more Tildy thought about it, the more ridiculous it began to seem to her. There was no real information except what Lucius had told her. If he were confronted with the tales he would surely deny everything. She began to feel angry at Lucius for creating such a problem in the first place and getting her involved with it. If only Papa were here and she could talk to him. He would surely know what to do about it. Then Tildy realized that the best thing to do would be to tell Mother. Mother was always so calm during almost any emergency. Surely Mother would know what to do.

Mother sat and listened very quietly to what Tildy had to say. Even as Tildy reported what Lucius said, it began to sound more and more unreasonable. She was glad she hadn't gone to Uncle Caleb or Aunt Rachel with such an outlandish tale.

When Tildy had finished, Mother took in a deep breath and then let it out slowly as she seemed to be thinking what to say.

"Suppose there really were such a plot," Mother said. "Can you imagine anyone letting a boy like Lucius know about it?"

Tildy couldn't help giggling. "Much less trusting him to carry a secret message of any importance!"

Mother laughed too, but Tildy detected more of pity and sadness than amusement about it.

"I remember now," Mother said. "When Lucius was so ill and I was changing the linens on his bed, I found some *penny dreadfuls* tucked away under his mattress. Perhaps he got some of his fanciful ideas from one of those books."

"You don't think he's crazy?" Tildy asked.

Mother took another very deep breath. "I don't think so. I think it's more that he's a product of the terrible times we've been living through. He let himself get so wrapped up in the South's cause and there was nothing he could actually do about it."

Tildy agreed sadly. "I'm afraid I taunted him once when he was boasting as he does. I teased him about the fact that he wasn't in the army."

"Oh, Tildy," Mother said and Tildy had no doubt that Mother was disappointed in her.

"I know, Mother, I shouldn't have done it. I was sorry immediately, but he can be so irritating and it just slipped out. Then later when I learned that he was not well, I just could have cut my tongue out."

Mother and Tildy sat silently for a while. Then Tildy asked, "Do you think we ought to talk to Aunt Rachel about it? About his saying there is a plan to harm the President?"

"It won't be at all easy," Mother said. "But I suppose I shall have to find a way to mention it to her. I'll do it as gently as I can."

"Thank you, Mother," Tildy said. "I can always count on you to pull my chestnuts out of the fire."

"I think it would be best for you to stay clear of Lucius," Mother said.

"Believe me, I try but sometimes I can't avoid him," Tildy said. "Won't it be lovely when we have a little house of our own?"

Later that day Tildy sat quietly with Mother in the parlor as they worked on their sewing. Tildy was certain that Mother was deep in her own thoughts. Maybe she was trying to think of a way to say what needed to be said to Aunt Rachel.

Tildy thought how complicated life could sometimes become. The last thing in the world Tildy had wanted was to get mixed up in some of Lucius' crazy ideas. Try as she might she could not seem to put it out of her mind. She remembered the way he had looked at her. There was something about the expression in Lucius' eyes when he had said, "It's true" that seemed so convincing.

A cold tingle slithered down Tildy's spine. Even if Lucius were crazy, there might be other crazy people who had just as hard a time as he did accepting the way the war had turned out. It was possible that there were people who might do strange, terrible things out of revenge or a misguided idea that they could change the outcome of events.

Tildy remembered that frightening story that Mother had told her about how men had threatened the Grahams one night after Papa had stumbled on their secret meeting in the woods. If she hadn't heard it from Mother's own lips Tildy would never have believed that such a thing could happen. Mother had told her that there were secret organizations of men who sympathized with the South.

Then Tildy thought of that newspaper that Lucius had and Uncle Caleb had gotten so upset about. Tildy had read in that paper about a man in the North who had been arrested for planning an uprising. An uprising of people in Indiana and Illinois. Lucius had told her something was going to happen in August. She had thought he had been delirious because of the fever when he raved on about that. But, somehow he had known of it.

Tildy hardly paid any attention when Mother said, "I just saw Rachel go up to her room. I think I'll see if I can talk to her in private there."

Tildy nodded absently as her mother left her alone in the parlor. Tildy remembered as though it had only happened yesterday how the Pettibones had come and painted that star on the Graham barn. Worse yet, she remembered that they had laughed and teased her and told her "not to let the 'Nu-Oh-Lac's get her." Mother had known about the secret password "Nu-Oh-Lac." So had that grubby-looking man that Lucius had talked to in Port Tobacco. And, Lucius had said that the Port Tobacco man was in on the plot. That man and others who came to Surratt's tavern and boardinghouse. Even Johnny Surratt and that actor John Wilkes Booth.

The more Tildy thought about it the crazier it seemed. And, the crazier it seemed, the more frightened Tildy became that it might really be true. What if those crazy people did have a real plan to harm the President? And, what if it sounded so crazy that no one did anything about it?

By the time it would take her to convince anybody that they should do something, it might be too late. Somebody had to act, but who? Tildy knew the answer deep in her own heart.

For a moment Tildy stood in the center of the parlor. Her sewing had fallen to the floor but she didn't notice it. All she could think of was that the President must be warned. How? What could she do? Then she remembered there were soldiers stationed at the Navy Yard Bridge. If only she could get a message to them. But who would take such a message?

Tildy ran to the cubbyhole under the hall stairs where the rag bag was kept. When she had collected costumes to enact her history lessons for the children she remembered seeing an old pair of Lucius' trousers in there. She dug through the pile of old clothing and linens, tossing aside in a heap anything that did not suit her needs. She was about to give up when she found what she had been looking for. The trousers were in poor condition, with torn knees, but Tildy didn't care. Glancing about to see that no one was watching, she slipped off her dress and petticoats and pulled on the trousers. She grabbed a shabby shirt that once must have been Uncle Caleb's. The sleeves were at least six inches too long but she rolled them up. She stuffed the shirttail inside the trousers. Then she ran to the back door and out to the barn. She snatched an old felt field hat off one of the hooks by the door. She jammed it on her head and pushed her hair up under it.

Inside the barn Tildy looked around, relieved to find that no one else was out there. Everything had happened so fast she had not had time to give any thought as to how she would explain what she was doing if Uncle Caleb or Lucius had been around.

Her relief turned to frustration, however, as she tried to find a saddle to put on Uncle Caleb's horse Brownie. Back home on the farm she had ridden Old Maud bareback many times, but she was afraid to try that on an animal she was not familiar with.

She heard a noise behind her and whirled guiltily. She sucked in her breath and then let it out again shakily, nearly crying she was so nervous.

"Cato! Thank goodness it's you," Tildy said.

"Look at you," he said. "How come you're dressed up like that?"

"I've got to have a horse right away," Tildy said. "But I can't find a saddle anywhere. Help me, Cato."

210

Cato backed away from her shaking his head. "Aw no, I can't do nothing like that without Master Caleb telling me I should do it."

"You've got to help me," Tildy demanded. "Something terrible is going to happen."

"Something terrible is gonna happen all right if Master Caleb finds out I been messing with his horse."

"You don't have to do anything except tell me where the saddle is," Tildy said. "I can take care of the rest."

Cato kept shaking his head stubbornly. "There'll be bad trouble."

"Listen to me, Cato," Tildy nearly shouted. "I have got to warn somebody that President Lincoln is in danger. Something terrible is going to happen unless I stop it. I've got to warn him."

"How are you gonna do that?"

"I don't know," Tildy was frantic at the time that was being wasted here. "Cato, do you want something terrible to happen to Mr. Lincoln?"

"No, ma'am!"

"It will unless I can get there in time," Tildy said, and then added. "Cato, if you don't help me get the saddle, I'll have to ride Brownie bareback."

"Oh, no! You mustn't try that. Brownie'd throw you off in a second."

"Please help me, Cato." Tears had started their way down Tildy's cheeks by now.

"I'll get the saddle," Cato said. "But we're in powerful bad trouble, I tell you truthful about that."

Together they got the horse saddled, even though Cato muttered the entire time about how much Uncle

211

Caleb had paid for this saddle and the terrible things that would happen if he ever found out they had taken it and the horse.

As they led Brownie from her stall, the horse whinnied and rolled her eyes.

"Help me up on her," Tildy begged.

"Brownie's looking mighty skittish," Cato said. "She don't like nobody but Mister Caleb or me to ride her."

"Then you'll have to come with me Cato. You get up in the saddle and pull me up behind you."

Cato hesitated.

Tildy surprised herself by shouting at him, "You do what I tell you, Cato. Right now!"

Cato responded to her command immediately and the two of them galloped out of the barn and through the lot toward the lane just as Uncle Caleb came up around the corner of the barn.

"What's going on here?" Uncle Caleb shouted. "Stop! Stop thief!"

The back door of the house slammed open and Lucius and Juno and Linny ran outside to see what the commotion was about.

"He's gonna kill us," Cato bellowed. "He's gonna skin us alive."

"Faster, Cato," Tildy shouted. "Faster, and don't you dare stop until I tell you to."

As they streaked down the lane toward the road, Tildy looked back and saw Mother and Aunt Rachel with the girls on the front verandah.

"Tildy! Is that you?" Mother called.

"I'll be back as soon as I can," Tildy shouted back to

her. "Don't worry. I know what I'm doing." She sounded far more confident than she actually was.

The horse pounded on down the road. Tildy clung to Cato's waist as she shouted instructions and encouragement in his ear.

"It's getting dark," Cato worried. "If this horse steps in a hole or stumbles she'll break her leg."

"Don't think about things like that," Tildy screamed at him. That was a worry she hadn't thought of. Fear bubbled up sourly in her throat.

"If this horse breaks her leg, Master Caleb will shoot her first and then us."

"Keep going Cato," Tildy said shrilly. "We can't stop now. We can't stop for anything. We'll be all right."

"Master Caleb gonna have my hide stretched out on the barn door," Cato wailed.

In desperation Tildy said, "Remember the story I read to you about Queen Matilda and how she escaped with one of her brave knights? Try to be courageous like that."

"I don't know courageous," Cato said.

"We're on an important mission to save the President. We're doing this for Mr. Lincoln."

Cato didn't answer but Tildy felt him gouge his knees in Brownie's side and the mare lunged forward faster than ever.

As they approached the Navy Yard Bridge, Tildy could see a small bonfire. The soldiers were huddled about it attempting to keep warm. She could hear them laughing and talking. A couple of them were shoving each other about in a playful fighting match. They scarcely glanced up as they galloped up and Cato reined in the horse.

"Please," Tildy called out to them. "Can someone help me?"

One of the men sauntered in her direction. "Well, now what have we got here?"

"I have an important message," Tildy said.

"And just who is this important message from?" the soldier enquired with a tone of amusement in his voice.

"This is about the President," Tildy said.

"Oh, you have an important message from Abe Lincoln, do you? And just why would he send a message with an out-at-the-knees young'un like you?"

By now some of the other soldiers had wandered over to join in the amusement.

"You've got to listen to me," Tildy insisted. "The President is in great danger. You've got to help me warn him."

"Well, of course we'll help." The soldier smirked as he winked broadly at one of the other guards. "What is it you want us to tell the President?"

"There's a plot to . . . to . . . " Tildy suddenly realized that she didn't know exactly what was supposed to happen. She did remember what Lucius had mentioned to her a while back about capturing the President to exchange him for Confederate prisoners.

"He's going to be kidnapped," Tildy cried.

The soldiers roared and howled at this bit of news.

"This isn't a laughing matter." Tildy knew she must have sounded as crazy to these soldiers as Lucius had sounded to her. She didn't know what she could do to make them understand.

"I'll tell you what," the soldier said, moving closer and reaching out toward the horse's bridle. "You come with me and I'll send one of these soldiers along with you to see that you get home safe and sound."

"Go, Cato! Go!," Tildy shouted. "We've got to get out of here."

This time Cato didn't argue with her. Obediently he kneed Brownie and they were off again. The horse's hooves thundered as they raced across the wooden bridge toward Washington.

The Capital city was alive with the signs of celebration. Most of the houses had lights in every window. The streets were full of people. It had been six days since the news of Lee's surrender had come through and people were still reveling.

"What'll we do now?" Cato asked Tildy.

She didn't have the slightest idea what to tell him.

"Let's dismount and give Brownie a rest while I think," she suggested.

Tildy's face burned as she thought about how the soldiers at the bridge had laughed at her story. It wouldn't do any good to try to get soldiers or anyone else to relay the message. She knew that the wise thing to do would be to give up and go back to Surrattsville. Who would listen to a couple of children?

Then Tildy knew who would listen. She thought of the things she had heard and read about how President Lincoln was a man of the people. He himself had come from common folks. He listened to people . . . all sorts of people. He had listened to mothers who had come to him to plead for their soldier sons. His door was opened to anyone. Tildy felt sure that if she could get to him he would hear her out. He wouldn't laugh.

"Get back in the saddle, Cato," Tildy said. "We're going to talk to Mr. Lincoln."

Again Cato did as he was told, reaching down to grab her hand and pull her up behind him.

"Where we gonna find Mr. Lincoln?" Cato asked.

Tildy was stumped for a moment and then she said, "We'll go to the President's house."

But try as she might, she could not think how to find it. She had only been in Washington two times in her life. Once when she and Mother and the girls had arrived on the train. The other time when Lucius had given them a brief sightseeing tour. That had been in the daytime, and at night everything looked very different. She hadn't the slightest idea where they were.

Tildy called to a man standing on the corner and asked him the way to the President's house, but the man was in no condition to give anyone directions. He was full of celebration.

Tildy tried several more times before she found someone who could tell her what she wanted to know. They started off through the streets. Tildy repeated the directions and street names as they went.

At last they saw it. A large white dwelling surrounded by tents and small bonfires such as the one they had seen at the bridge. Cato and Tildy rode right up to the front door of the President's mansion. All the time she tried to work out in her mind just what it was that she would say. She would have to be very careful so that they didn't get the same reception they had received at the bridge.

A soldier was on guard at the door. Tildy slid down from Brownie's back and walked up to the guard.

"I beg your pardon," she said as calmly as she could. "I need to speak to the President."

The soldier looked down at her and as she looked up at him she saw that he had soft gray eyes. They reminded her of Papa's.

"I'm sorry, but the President is not at home this evening. Would you care to leave a message?"

Tildy looked up at him again to make sure that he wasn't laughing at her the way the soldiers had at the bridge. His expression was very serious.

For a moment Tildy was tempted to tell him what she wanted, but then she decided that she could not risk it.

"No," she said quietly. "No message."

She started to leave but then turned back. "Do you know when the President will be home to receive visitors?"

"No, I don't know that. He and Mrs. Lincoln went to the theater tonight."

"The theater?"

"Yes. They went to Ford's Theater. If you want to get a look at him, you might wait outside. You could see him when he comes out after the play is over."

"And where would I find the theater?" Tildy asked.

"Ford's Theater is on 10th Street between 'E' and 'F.'" The guard gave her careful instructions about how to find it. He even helped Tildy up onto the horse behind Cato.

"Go fast as you can, Cato," Tildy called out. "There's still time."

They galloped urgently through the streets trying vainly to follow the directions the guard had given them. Their very haste made them lose their way more than once. Every wrong turn they took increased the ominous sense of apprehension in Tildy's mind.

When at last they managed to arrive at 10th Street, they found their way blocked by swarms of people. At first Tildy thought these were merely celebrating crowds that had spilled over into this thoroughfare. Then she realized that the sounds she heard were not sounds of joy or happiness. This was the clamor of shock and confusion. People, in a state of disbelief and horror, were milling about aimlessly. Everyone was talking at once to no one in particular.

"What's happening?" Tildy cried out. "What is going on here?"

No one paid any attention to her. Everyone seemed wrapped in a numb cocoon.

She half-slid, half-fell off Brownie's back and went over to a man dressed in a fine frock coat and a tall beaver hat. She tugged on his sleeve.

"What is the matter?" She said insistently.

The man looked down at her. His face seemed ghostly white against the night sky. His eyes had a glazed appearance.

"Don't you know?" the man asked. "It's the President. He has been shot."

Tildy took a step backward as the full impact of what he had said hit her.

The man continued talking, as much to himself as to Tildy, but she heard him say, "It was John Wilkes Booth who shot President Lincoln."

Tildy reached out for support as her knees sagged weakly beneath her. No one seemed to be paying any attention to her. She sank down on a mounting block at the edge of the street.

The recollection of the face of the man that Anna Surratt had hidden behind that picture on her mantle seemed to hover in front of Tildy's eyes. She covered her face with her hands. "Lucius said they were going to capture the President," she moaned.

Cato jumped down from the horse and holding onto the reins sat beside her. The two of them sat side by side and wept.

At last Cato asked, "What're we gonna do now?"

"I don't know, Cato. I guess it's all over. We got here too late."

"We didn't do no good," Cato said.

Tildy nodded. Cato was right. It had all been for nothing. Hadn't Mother said to her that Tildy often took on more than she could actually accomplish? She should have known better than to think she could have warned the President in time.

"We're failures," Cato moaned.

Suddenly Tildy stood up and said to him, "No, we're not failures."

It was almost as though she heard Papa's voice reminding her of something she had nearly forgotten. "The only failures are the people who don't even try."

Cato looked up at her. He seemed to be trying to understand.

"Don't you see? We tried. We tried as hard as we could to help. We did everything it was possible for us to do."

Cato stood up. "I expect we best be getting home now."

"You're right," she said.

He clambered up on Brownie's back. Tildy used the mounting block to help her climb behind him.

"What do you suppose will happen when we get back?"

"I don't know," Tildy said. "Are you scared?"

"Yep," Cato said, nodding. "But not as scared as before, 'cause I know we tried to do what was right. We did the best we could."

Tildy said, "You're right. We tried." Then she seemed to hear Papa's reassuring voice in the back of her mind, repeating the familiar words right along with her. "We did the best we could. That's all anybody can expect us to do."

As Cato nudged Brownie's flank with his heels they started to move away from the city. Tildy looked back. She knew that she would never forget this night and all that had happened as long as she lived.

In some strange way that she could not quite explain, she knew that this bitter disappointment would make her a stronger person. She knew that no matter what happened to her in the years to come, she would be able to face anything because of this.

Both Mr. Lincoln and Papa had given their lives for what they had believed in. Their strength and courage would always be with her. The brown thrush would sing in her heart, forever.

S
367-7620

H
491-8708